D0015861

⇾ finally, ⇽
SOMETHING MYSTERIOUS

DOUG CORNETT

WITHDRAWN

ALFRED A. KNOPF NEW YORK

THIS IS A BORZOI BOOK PUBLISHED BY ALFRED A. KNOPF

This is a work of fiction. Names, characters, places, and incidents either are the product of the author's imagination or are used fictitiously. Any resemblance to actual persons, living or dead, events, or locales is entirely coincidental.

Text copyright © 2020 by Doug Cornett
Jacket art copyright © 2020 by Ellen Duda
Map art copyright © 2020 by Ellen Duda

All rights reserved. Published in the United States by Alfred A. Knopf, an imprint of Random House Children's Books, a division of Penguin Random House LLC, New York.

Knopf, Borzoi Books, and the colophon are registered trademarks of Penguin Random House LLC.

Visit us on the Web! rhcbooks.com

Educators and librarians, for a variety of teaching tools, visit us at RHTeachersLibrarians.com

Library of Congress Cataloging-in-Publication Data
Names: Cornett, Doug, author.
Title: Finally, something mysterious / Doug Cornett.
Description: First edition. | New York : Alfred A. Knopf, [2020] | Summary: In a small California town during the summer between fifth and sixth grade, three children investigate when hundreds of rubber duckies show up in Mr. Babbage's backyard.
Identifiers: LCCN 2018060575 | ISBN 978-1-9848-3003-6 (hardcover) | ISBN 978-1-9848-3004-3 (lib. bdg.) | ISBN 978-1-9848-3005-0 (ebook)
Subjects: | CYAC: Mystery and detective stories. | Summer—Fiction.
Classification: LCC PZ7.1.C6728 Fi 2020 | DDC [Fic]—dc23

The text of this book is set in 12-point Bell Monotype.
Interior design by Trish Parcell

Printed in the United States of America
April 2020
10 9 8 7 6 5 4 3 2 1

First Edition

Random House Children's Books supports the First Amendment and celebrates the right to read.

⇒ finally, ⇐
SOMETHING MYSTERIOUS

To Leo and Anna

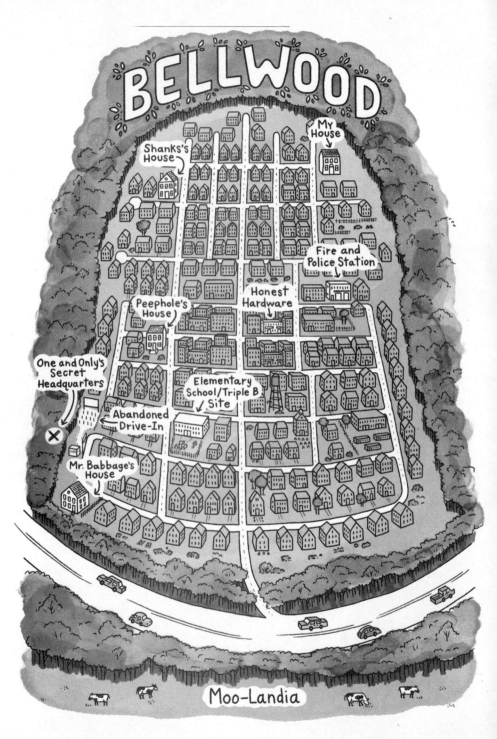

The First Weird Thing

The weirdness in Bellwood all began with the smoke in the air and the ducks in Mr. Babbage's backyard. After they showed up, a lot of other weird things started happening. Mysteries, you could call them. Some of them were scratch-your-head-and-say-hmm kind of weird, but a couple of them were big-time weird. Stare-up-at-the-night-sky-and-wonder-about-the-meaning-of-life kind of weird. And-hope-that-while-I'm-staring-up-there-a-bird-does-not-poop-on-me-cuz-that-would-not-be-a-good-sign-regarding-the-meaning-of-life. That kind of weird.

The smoke was easy to explain: a wildfire was burning in a big state forest outside of town. When the wind shifted the wrong way, all of Bellwood smelled like a campfire.

The ducks in Babbage's yard were a different story. They appeared one seemingly normal Tuesday morning, scattered all over the grass. There must have been hundreds of them, their little yellow tails poking into the air, each duck with the same creepy look on its face: eyes wide open and vacant, like empty garages; bill curved upward in a kind of lipsticked maniac smile. I could picture the moment Babbage discovered them: he looks out at his backyard as he drinks his morning coffee, then *boom*—his mouth gapes open, his eyes go wonky, his coffee mug drops to the ground. *Crash. Splash.* Duckies? Duckies!

These were rubber duckies—the kind you take a bath with. Nobody could explain where they came from. None of his neighbors had ducks in their backyards. But Babbage's yard? Overrun with ducks. A mystery.

News spread quickly in Bellwood. A dog could barf up an action figure on one side of town, and before it was mopped up, people would be debating the finer points of canine digestion on the other side of town. I know because that actually happened. Don't believe me? Ask my dog, Ronald. But that's what you get for living in such a small, out-of-the-way place. And so when rubber duckies invaded Babbage's yard, everybody knew about it, and fast. By ten in the morning, the One and Onlys—that's my two best friends and me—were racing our bikes up the cul-de-sacs of Bellwood, cutting through backyards, and trundling through woods, hoping to get there before the little visitors vanished.

Shanks, Peephole, and I made the crosstown trek in exceptionally good time (apologies to Mrs. Hoover's geraniums, may they RIP) and rolled up to a clump of stupefied

Bellwoodians staring at the ducks with wary eyes. Mr. Babbage's dog, a little white yappy thing, was bouncing around the yard, growling wildly at the ducks. Officer Portnoy, who had just visited our fifth-grade classroom on the last day of school to remind us about proper bicycle safety, was talking to Mr. Babbage at the edge of the lawn. Portnoy held a duck inches from his face. It looked like they were having a staring contest. The duck was winning.

"Okay, One and Onlys," Shanks said. "Time to gather clues. Paul, you go snoop on Mr. Babbage and Officer Portnoy. See if you can overhear anything that might be useful. Peephole and I will get a closer look at these duckies."

I strolled over and stood behind Babbage and Officer Portnoy, trying to appear like a normal, nonsnooping kid.

"Well, Mr. Baggage," I heard Officer Portnoy say, "I'm stymied."

"Please, call me Lance," Babbage said, nervously smoothing the collar of his bathrobe and shifting his gaze from his transformed backyard to the growing crowd of onlookers.

Mr. Babbage was always very well dressed, and today was no exception. His bathrobe was scarlet and silky, and it went all the way down to his feet, which were clad in slippers made of some kind of animal fur. His thin black hair was parted perfectly to one side, and his thick eyebrows seemed to be combed.

"You don't think they're . . . dangerous, do you?" I heard him ask Officer Portnoy, his face tight with worry.

Officer Portnoy shook his head and clapped Babbage on

the back. "They're not *real* ducks," he said in a reassuring tone. "So no need to worry."

But Babbage did look worried. He flicked his eyes back and forth to see if anybody was listening, but luckily he didn't look down at me. He leaned closer to Officer Portnoy. He began whispering something, so I casually inched up behind them to listen.

". . . and normally I wouldn't pay attention to such things. It's just that it was so vivid . . . so *real*. In my dream, there was a horrible beast in my backyard . . . an enormous, ghastly . . . *thing*. . . ." Babbage's voice was faint and wavering. "It was trying to get in my house, you see, but I wouldn't open the door. Its breath was heavy, steady— almost like a machine. *Chuk chuk chuk*. The walls were rattling. And then I woke up, and I could have sworn, for a second or two, that I still heard it breathing, but faint, like it had already run away. And that's when I looked out the window and saw . . . *them*." He nodded at the ducks. "I called the police immediately—didn't even go outside to look. I just had this spooky feeling about them. It must be some kind of sign, don't you think?"

Portnoy shrugged, never taking his eyes off the duckies. "I'm afraid dreams are out of my jurisdiction."

Meanwhile, Shanks had wandered into the middle of the yard and was standing among a litter of ducks, grinning from ear to ear, her arms outstretched. Compared with the ducks, and with Mr. Babbage's dog, Shanks looked like a giant, which is maybe why she was smiling so much, because in reality she was short. Shortest-person-in-the-fifth-grade short, and unless she was planning on growing a bunch over the summer or somebody else was planning on shrinking, she'd be the shortest person in the sixth grade, too. Sometimes when we all hung out together, people mistook her for Peephole's little sister, which Peephole thought was hilarious. Shanks didn't.

Shanks may have been small, but her personality was big. Like right now, she was having a blast in Babbage's backyard. Her electric-blond hair, almost white, which cascaded over her shoulders and reached down to her lower back, was swishing to and fro as she surveyed all the little yellow bodies around her. Shanks was like me: she *loved* mysteries.

Peephole, meanwhile, lingered at the edge of the crowd. He liked solving things, but mysteries made him uncomfortable. Actually, a lot of things made him uncomfortable: thunder, black ice, cats, leftovers, gym class, Vikings, loose tree branches that could fall on you at any time, eating outside, athlete's foot, certain cheeses, girls, basketball, the sound of other people's sneezes, the bubonic plague, Norwegian accents, and nose hair trimmers, to name a few. Worst of all, Peephole was afraid of bugs. And if you squinted, the duckies sort of looked like an infestation.

Babbage smoothed his collar again. "I guess I'm just on edge. This smoke"—he sniffed the air—"it's so . . . eerie."

Officer Portnoy clicked his tongue in agreement, then

turned to the crowd with a little startle, as if these thirty or so people had suddenly snuck up on him. Not exactly the most perceptive person, especially for a police officer.

"Okay, everyone, go on home. Nothing to see here."

Whenever there is clearly something very interesting to see, adults say there is "nothing to see." It must be in the manuals for police officers and teachers.

Officer Portnoy noticed me looking up at him. A silence hung in the air between us. Finally, he said, "Macaroni."

"Marconi," I corrected him. I love mac and cheese, but I don't want to be mistaken for it.

"Pam Macaroni."

Oh, come on. Bellwood's finest was not exactly Sherlock Holmes. "Paul, actually."

"Right. So, Paul . . . are you practicing proper bicycle safety?" He grinned down at me. Or, rather, the giant mustache that almost entirely covered his mouth grinned down at me.

I thought of the poor toad sculpture in the Lombardis' yard, the one that I had decapitated in my mad rush to get there. RIP to you, too, Mr. Toad. "For the most part," I answered.

"Glad to hear it. Safety comes first. Always remember that. Now, Paul, there's nothing to see—"

"Can I take one?"

Officer Portnoy seemed surprised by my question. I was, too. I didn't know I was going to ask it until it came out.

"A duck? Why?"

What I was thinking: *Because nobody knew why they had shown up here in Babbage's backyard. Because they could have come from anywhere. Because each little yellow rubber ducky was a tiny, crazy, perfect little mystery.*

What I said: "Because I lost mine. You know, I haven't been able to take a bath since."

"Is that so?" Portnoy turned to look at the yard. I followed his gaze: Peephole was now sitting cross-legged on the ground with his back to the duckies, dabbing sweat from his forehead with his T-shirt. Even from here, he looked nauseous. "Is your friend all right?"

"Peephole? Yeah, he's fine. Just has a fear of rubber duckies."

Portnoy let out a tiny I-give-up sigh. "What kind of name is 'Peephole'?"

A fair question. Surprise, surprise, Peephole's name was not really Peephole (nobody's parents are *that* mean). His birth name was Alexander Calloway, but only adults still called him Alexander. You see, he was the tallest and skinniest kid in the class, and he was a little touchy about it. He and Shanks looked pretty goofy standing side by side, but some things are worth looking goofy for, and friendship is one of them.

In fourth grade, we had a teacher named Mr. Pocus, who was nobody's favorite. He was permanently grouchy, as if every single morning he poured rotten milk on his

Cheerios to keep himself mean. Once I thought I saw a picture of him smiling, but then I realized it was upside down. He was also the "chief taster" in our town's annual bratwurst competition, which made him both feared and respected.

For some reason, Mr. Pocus had it out for Alexander. I suspected it was because he was jealous of Peephole's height. Pocus was short, and if you put a studded collar and a leash on him, he'd look just like a cartoon bulldog. He had this nickname for Alexander, "Beanpole," which he called him because Alexander was so tall and lanky—like a beanstalk, I guess. Pocus always used to call him up to the board to solve the hardest math problems, like he really wanted him to get them wrong in front of everybody. But Alexander would always get the answers right, which annoyed Mr. Pocus even more.

One day during math class, Alexander had a bad head cold and his nose was all stuffed up. He had been speaking with that snotty voice that people get when their sinuses are clogged. As if sensing weakness, Mr. Pocus was particularly ruthless. "Beanpole this," and "Beanpole that." You could tell that Alexander was getting upset because his face had turned a shade of red I'd only ever seen in a sixty-four-box of crayons.

Mr. Pocus called him up to the board to do a hard problem, and I mean *really* hard. It was a story problem about this guy named Theodore, who had a super-complicated trip to the grocery store. We're talking fractions, coupons, remainders—even a spill in aisle nine. I was completely lost, and I wasn't the only one; the girl next to me, Jessie Futterman, fainted from confusion.

Alexander stood up there, squinting at the board, swaying back and forth, his arms hanging down like pool noodles, a piece of chalk gripped in his fingers.

"Give up, Beanpole?" Mr. Pocus sneered. "Did I get you this time, Beanpole?"

Alexander turned his head slowly and glared at Mr. Pocus. Then he raised the piece of chalk and, with a few swift movements, wrote his answer.

Mr. Pocus made a sour-milk face. Alexander got it right!

Triumphantly, Alexander wheeled around to face the class and announced, in a proud, high, bold, and nasally voice, *"My name is not Beanpole!"*

Except that his nose was so stuffed up that it came out as *"By dame biz dot Peephole!"*

Well, nobody called him Beanpole after that. But Peephole—that one stuck.

I wasn't about to explain all this to Portnoy. Besides, his attention had shifted and he was watching Shanks, who was doing some kind of ballet dance in the middle of the duckies and giving a speech to them. Suddenly, she twisted around to face us. "It's wet!" she cried out.

"What is?" I called back.

"The grass!" She did a little arm-pump dance. "A clue!"

I turned to Portnoy, who looked confused. "Don't you think that's odd?" I asked.

He nodded. "She seems very odd."

"No, I mean the grass. It's wet!"

"Wet grass? Why would that be odd?"

"Because we're in the middle of a drought. It hasn't rained in weeks."

"Oh, yeah." He looked a little embarrassed that he hadn't thought of that. "Well, Babbage could have watered his lawn with a sprinkler this morning."

I swept my eyes across the backyard. "I don't see a sprinkler. Besides, he said he woke up from his dream about the monster, saw the ducks, and called the police without even going outside. He wouldn't have had *time* to water his lawn."

Portnoy shot me a sideways glance that was somewhere between impressed and annoyed. "So you were listening in on my conversation with him, huh?" He turned back to the lawn and frowned; Shanks had picked up an armful of ducks and was waltzing with them.

"Oh, don't mind Shanks," I said, eager to change the subject. "She's a little . . . out there."

"Shanks? What kind of name—" Portnoy began, but then he shook his head. He had a look in his eye that made him seem unsure. About the duckies, me, this lunatic world we live in. His mustache, though, was unflappable.

Shanks's honest-to-God full birth name: Gloria Longshanks Hill. Apparently, Mr. and Mrs. Hill believed that when it came to middle names, the stranger the better.

(Rumor had it that Shanks's mom's middle name was "Lady Dragonslayer," but I was never able to confirm this.) Well, Mr. and Mrs. Hill were both pretty big history buffs, and their favorite time period was medieval England, because nobody back then was named just Dave or Jen. They had awesome names, like King Edward the First, aka the Hammer of the Scots, aka King Longshanks. They called him Longshanks because he was tall, and "shanks" was what people used to call legs. I always found it funny that Shanks was named after somebody so tall. Shanks didn't.

But nobody called Shanks "Gloria," not even Shanks herself. Shanks was a Shanks, if there ever was one.

Me? I was just Paul. To be honest, I was a little jealous of Peephole and Shanks. I'd secretly always wanted a cool nickname, but nothing ever came up. I guess every group needs a person with no nickname, just to keep it grounded.

Portnoy turned his attention back to me and cleared his throat with a guttural noise that sounded like a heavy-duty vacuum cleaner trying to work through a massive clog of dog hair. "I can appreciate that you want a keepsake from this little spectacle, but the ducks are officially evidence now. They belong in the storage shed next to the police department." His face fell a little when he said that, as if he had realized that he would actually have to gather all these ducks up by hand and transport them to the police station. He gazed down at me. "Paul"—he struggled for the right words—"they're not real."

He smiled and patted the top of my head, which made

me feel like a toddler. I wondered how clueless he thought I was.

"I figured that much out," I said patiently. "I thought it would be cool to keep one."

"I don't have any problem with you taking one, Paul, but if I gave *you* a rubber ducky, then I'd have to give one to your friends, Pebble and Chunk, and *everyone* else out here, and then there wouldn't be any evidence left. Would there?" His face softened, and he patted my head again. "They're just ordinary old duckies, son. Now, if you'll excuse me, I've got a crowd to control."

With that, he began to shoo the onlookers away from Babbage's yard, waving the air in front of him like he was walking into a flock of pigeons. I started making my way toward Shanks, but a voice called to me from behind.

"Paul Marconi? Is that you?"

I whirled around to see Janice Wagner, my neighbor from across the street. Janice was a sophomore in high school, and she used to babysit me when I was small. She was a great babysitter, really funny and willing to play any stupid game I came up with, and she had a trampoline in her backyard that she let me jump on once or twice, even though my parents said I wasn't supposed to. She was cool like that, but we hadn't spoken for a couple of years.

"Oh my *gosh*," she said, clasping a hand to her mouth and trying to stifle a giggle. Her short black hair bounced around her narrow face, and her pine-tree-green eyes looked at me in disbelief. "You're not a little kid anymore!"

I grinned, and then felt embarrassed at how big I was grinning, so I clasped a hand over my mouth. "Nope, I'm not," I mumbled, which sounded weird, so I said, "Yes, I'm not," which sounded even weirder.

Sometimes talking can be hard.

Janice had one foot up on a motorized scooter, and she was wearing an enormous black bag on her back. It sort of made her look like a human-sized snail with a huge shell.

She noticed me noticing the bag. "My tuba," she explained, with a thumb point over her shoulder. "A few of us band geeks have been selected to play the victory song when they announce the Bellwood Bratwurst Bonanza winner this weekend. It's sort of a big deal. I was just on my way to practice when I saw all these ducks. . . ."

"That *is* a big deal," I agreed, because it really was. The Bellwood Bratwurst Bonanza—or Triple B, for short— was the biggest party of the year in our little town. For Bellwoodians, it was like New Year's Eve in Times Square times a thousand, with sausages.

"It's an honor just to be a part of it." A curly-haired kid with freckles who was holding a trombone inserted himself into our conversation. It was Chad Foster, who was my age but happened to be the best trombone player in Bellwood. Once, on a dare, Chad ate seven cafeteria cupcakes in five minutes, then passed out during gym class. It was hard for me to take him seriously after that.

"It should be a great Triple B this year," he continued.

"One for the history books. Your parents are always contenders, Marconi. But there's no denying that Babbage here is at the top of his game. Can anybody dethrone him? It would take a herculean effort, that's for sure." He put a thoughtful finger on his chin. When not practicing the trombone, he spent most of his free time watching sports on TV, which is why he sounded like an announcer at a football game. "Going to be a close one this year, a real barn burner. I'll bet you dollars to donuts that this Triple B will be the most competitive in history. At this point, it's anybody's Bonanza!"

Peephole and Shanks appeared at my side and nodded hellos to Janice and Chad. Janice and Chad nodded back. We must have looked like a bunch of bobblehead dolls, standing around in silence as the crowd bustled past us.

"So this is pretty weird," Janice said, looking out over the ducks on Babbage's lawn.

"Weird and awesome," Shanks said, beaming. "Anybody have any clue where they came from?"

"Nope." Chad shuffled his feet. "But *he* seems pretty happy about it." He pointed his trombone across the lawn to the tall wooden fence that separated Babbage's yard from his neighbor's. There was a face peeking over the fence, smiling at the mess with wicked amusement. It was a leering, twisted little face.

"Oh, no. It's *him*," Peephole groaned.

The scowl above the fence belonged to Mr. Pocus.

Apparently, Mr. Babbage and the cruelest teacher in Bellwood were neighbors.

"They don't get much meaner than that," Chad said. "I heard that once, a long time ago, Pocus was so awful to a student that the kid flipped out, ran out of the classroom, and moved to Antarctica that night."

"Antarctica is really far away," Peephole said. "Lucky kid."

"There's no way that happened," I protested. "You don't just up and move to Antarctica, no matter how big of a jerk your teacher is."

"Paul's right," Janice said. At last, the voice of reason. "He didn't move to Antarctica that night. He stayed in bed for a month and refused to go back to school. And *then* he moved to Antarctica."

"You can refuse to go to school?" Peephole asked, surprised. "I wish I had known that when Pocus was my teacher." He glared across the lawn at Pocus with a mix of anger and fear, as if Pocus might notice him at any moment and call him up to the board.

"At least that's what I heard," Janice said. "The kid was a few years older than me. Oh! Byron! Maybe you'd know!" Janice reached out and grabbed the arm of an impossibly tall teenager walking by. The kid had long fiery red hair, and he leaned over our circle like a streetlight. "Did you have Mr. Pocus? Did you hear about the kid whose life he ruined?"

Byron tugged at his thick bun of red hair, as if he was

already bored with the conversation. "I don't know," he said, his eyes flicking to Pocus's face peering over the fence. "You can't waste your time on grumps like him. Life's too short."

"How come you looked at me when you said 'short'?" Shanks said accusingly.

"You're Byron Willis," Peephole interjected, looking up at him. It was rare for Peephole to look up at anybody. "You're the chief of the Bellwood Junior Firefighters."

"That's right," Byron said.

"You're tall," Peephole added.

"Yep," Byron said. "So are you."

"Thanks," Peephole said.

"Brilliant conversation," Shanks muttered under her breath.

Again a few seconds of silence settled on our circle, which was finally broken by Portnoy's gruff voice announcing there was "nothing to see here."

With that, we joined the gawkers of Bellwood as they dispersed to their cars and their homes and their ordinary old summer day.

But I knew better. These weren't ordinary old duckies, and this was *not* an ordinary old day in Bellwood.

2

Our Investigation Begins!

"**W**hat should we call him?" Shanks held a little ducky in the palm of her hand. She'd swiped it from Babbage's yard when no one was looking.

"How about 'Mister E'?" I suggested, snatching the ducky from her.

"I wouldn't touch that thing," Peephole said. "We don't know where it came from. For all we know, Mr. Babbage's dog could have licked it. Do you know how many germs are in a dog's mouth? Do you know that my aunt Minnie's pug eats its own poo?"

"First of all, that's disgusting," I said. "Second, this is a clue, and detectives can't be scared of clues. Now, where did you come from, Mister E?"

I turned the ducky over and it answered me. Sort of. DUNNING TOY COMPANY was stamped on the bottom. I showed Peephole and Shanks.

"That doesn't tell us very much," Peephole said.

"But it's a lead," Shanks added optimistically.

The three of us were reviewing the facts of the case from the safety of our secret headquarters, which was only two blocks from Babbage's house, in a thin patch of woods on the edge of an overgrown field that had once been a drive-in movie theater. It wasn't much of a headquarters, just a simple lean-to that we had built the summer before with some sticks and tree branches, but it was tucked away in a part of town that nobody ever seemed to come to. I'd etched ONE AND ONLYS with a knife onto a piece of lumber from my dad's hardware store and had nailed it to the trunk of the tree that the lean-to was built against. It was where the One and Onlys always met to discuss our cases. It was our lair, our fortress, and nobody else knew about it, not even our parents.

My attention drifted from Mister E to the abandoned drive-in movie screen in the field in front of us. It was huge and had discolored from white to a dingy shade of brown, and there were wild vines growing up the side of it. The theater hadn't shown a movie for decades, but my dad told me that when he was a kid everybody in Bellwood would go out on Friday and Saturday nights to the drive-in. I sort of felt bad for the lonely old screen, being abandoned like that. But I knew that was stupid.

"So you're saying that all those duckies shot up from the sewer?" Peephole was doing his best to understand Shanks's line of logic. "Like, a volcano of bath toys?"

Shanks scrunched up her nose and stuck her lower lip out. Her eyes went a little bit crossed. This was her deep-in-thought face. "I'm saying they *could* have. You guys saw it, didn't you—the manhole cover in Mr. Babbage's backyard?"

I had noticed it, and I knew it meant that the sewer line ran directly below the backyard. But the manhole cover was still in place, which meant that if somehow those duckies came from underground, then someone, or something, had to have put the cover back on.

"Okay," Peephole continued, "so let's say they came from the sewer. Then how did they get down there?"

"How does anything get down there?"

"Somebody flushed hundreds of rubber duckies down their toilet?"

Shanks's mouth curled upward stubbornly. "I didn't say that it *did* happen that way. Just that it *could* have. We have to keep every possibility open until we're able to rule it out." The thing about Shanks and Peephole was that, even though they were best friends, they bickered all the time. Usually it was my job to referee their conversations.

"Babbage's grass was wet, and it hasn't rained in days," I said, but I didn't have to remind them of that. The tinge of smoke in the air was enough to remind us all of the wildfires raging outside of town. "I have a feeling that's the key to this mystery. If we can figure out why his grass was wet, then we'll know where the duckies came from."

Peephole and Shanks contemplated this for a moment.

"Maybe Mr. Babbage put them all there," Peephole said. He was always suspicious of people. The only few he trusted were his parents, Shanks, and me. That was why he rode his bike to school—he was convinced the bus driver was going to kidnap him and drive him to a work camp in Nebraska.

"An inside job?" Shanks pulled her hair against her face so that it looked like a beard. She did this whenever she was working through a particularly puzzling idea. "Interesting theory."

"Why would he put hundreds of rubber ducks in his yard, then call the cops?" I asked.

Shanks scratched her head and said, "You know how some people take all their clothes off and run out onto the field during the World Series?"

Peephole and I looked at each other, confused.

"What I'm saying is, people do strange things for attention."

I was skeptical. "Babbage was spooked. I overheard him telling Officer Portnoy about a nightmare he had right before the ducks appeared. He said it sounded like something . . . a monster . . . was trying to get into his house. Did you see the way he was gawking at the ducks? He looked downright terrified."

Peephole turned pale. "Adults dream about monsters, too?"

"So if Babbage didn't do it, then somebody put those ducks in his yard for a reason," I said. "But who? And why?"

"No idea," Shanks sighed. Then her face became serious. "But maybe whoever did it was there this morning in the crowd. Don't criminals often return to the scene of the crime?"

"It's not really a crime scene," Peephole said in a nasally voice.

"Fine. Maybe whoever did it returned to the scene of the *weirdness*. So who was there at Babbage's?"

I wracked my brain to remember. There had been a pretty decent crowd, with a lot of faces peering at the ducks. I hated to admit it, but I had been so distracted by the sea of yellow that I forgot to notice who was there. I had a long way to go to becoming a master detective. But the One and Onlys had a secret weapon: Peephole's photographic memory. Now his chin was tilted up and his eyes were flicking back and forth, like he was watching a Ping-Pong match in the sky or trying to ward off a sneeze.

Finally, he spoke. "There were twenty-three people there, including us, Babbage, and Officer Portnoy. Out of the other eighteen, I only recognized seven people. They were Dr. Momani, the dentist; Chad Foster, the trombone player from our class; Darrel Sullivan, the . . . uh . . . guy with the bleached-white goatee; Missy What's-Her-Name, the high school basketball player; Steph Something-or-Other, Missy What's-Her-Name's friend, who plays a sport, too, but I'm not sure if it's basketball or soccer or—"

"Not important," Shanks interrupted. "Keep going."

Peephole looked hurt, but he went on with the list.

"Byron Willis, the Junior Firefighter; Janice Wagner, who plays tuba in the high school band and who lives right across the street from Paul."

"Who else?" Shanks was impatient to get through the list.

"A lot of people I didn't know: a teenage guy with a shaved head and sunglasses; another teenager with big black boots and a green cast on her left arm; a little kid with his pants on backward, which I thought was a mistake, but then I thought, *Maybe that's the style these days for little kids*; the little kid's dad, whose hat was on backward, so maybe it just runs in the family; a big old lady whose face was so wrinkly it almost looked like a mask, holding the hand of a little girl with blond hair and a voice like a squirrel on helium; a short guy with skunk hair; a tall lady with . . ."

Shanks and I exchanged a glance as Peephole continued his report. We both were thinking the same thing: there was no way we could investigate all those people.

Finally, Peephole's list came to an end, and he beamed at us with a proud grin.

"You forgot somebody," I said.

Peephole frowned. "I never forget."

"Pocus was there, too," I reminded him. "He was watching from over the fence between his yard and Babbage's."

"Oh, yeah," Peephole admitted. "I guess I blocked him out."

"Maybe we should be thinking about motive, instead," Shanks suggested. "Like, who would *want* to dump duckies all over Babbage's yard?"

"I don't know about that, but I do know that Babbage was rattled by it. Maybe that's what the person intended," I said.

"But who would want to scare poor Babbage?" Peephole asked. "He's never done anything except make delicious bratwurst dishes year after year."

"As far as we know," Shanks said. "Maybe he's got a dark past that he keeps a secret."

"Or maybe somebody got tired of losing to him at the Triple B every year," I suggested.

Shanks pointed at me, a gleam in her eye. "You may be onto something! That's an angle we should investigate." She reached out and put her fist in the middle of our circle. "The One and Onlys are on the case!"

Peephole put his fist on top of Shanks's, and I put mine on top of Peephole's. Then all three of us opened our hands and made explosion noises.

The One and Onlys was the name we gave ourselves because we were each an only child. The One and Onlys had investigated our first case on the day we all met. It was the start of fourth grade, and the three of us found ourselves at the back of the lunch line. Peephole, who was still "Alexander" then, was in front of me, looking really nervous. Sweating, biting his lip, staring up at the food counter. I recognized him from my class, and so I asked him what was wrong.

"If I tell you, you'll laugh," he said sheepishly.

"No, I won't," I said. "Promise."

He shrugged. "I have a fear of school lunches."

I didn't laugh. But the short girl with electric-blond hair behind me did. I recognized her from our class, too.

"What do you think will happen?" she asked. "It'll try to eat you back?"

By the time we got our lunches, every table but one was full, so we had to sit together. As we poked at our food with our plastic sporks, we tried to guess what the main dish was. The lunch lady had called it chicken, but it was definitely not chicken. It was *chicken-like*, but there was something about it that reminded us of fish and dog food and (weirdly) mulch. Shanks examined the "chicken" with a magnifying glass that she retrieved from her backpack. That's the moment I knew we were going to be friends. Anybody who brings a magnifying glass to the first day of school obviously shares my love of solving mysteries. Peephole was less interested in the mystery and more concerned that the stench of the lunch might make him sick. That's Peephole in a nutshell right there. I offered him my backpack to throw up in. The three of us got so distracted that we were late getting back to class.

The results of our first investigation were inconclusive, but we all resolved to bring our lunch from home from then on. And thus the One and Onlys were born. Since then, we'd investigated several puzzling things, like the Case of the Missing TV Remote, the Case of the Class Hamster's Lost Tail, and the Case of Why Is Mr. Pocus Such a Butthead?

I was the hound dog of our team, the one who sniffed out the mysteries, because I had a nose for unusual things. Shanks was the muscle, completely unafraid of anything or anyone. Peephole had his photographic memory, but aside from that, he was mostly along for the ride because . . . what else was he going to do? He was a little sensitive about his value to our team. I mean, he *wanted* to be useful, but most of the time he was preoccupied by trying not to hurl. Let's be honest . . . Peephole wasn't exactly the bravest of sleuths. But the three of us had each other's backs, and that was the most important thing.

But soon Peephole wouldn't be a One and Only anymore. He was going to be a big brother, and considering the eleven-year age difference, a *really* big brother. And that meant that he'd have to babysit and help more around the house. And that meant that he probably wouldn't have time to run around town, solving mysteries with Shanks and me. He was going to have to be responsible. And guess what? It scared him.

To be honest, it sort of scared me, too. If Peephole was too busy to solve mysteries with us, would Shanks and I still do it? Soon Peephole was going to be a big brother and we were all going to be middle schoolers. Would we be too old to be detectives?

I carefully placed Mister E on the top of our lean-to, like a tiny little guard. Then we mounted our bikes and pedaled through the woods and out into the tall grass near the abandoned drive-in. There was a white pickup truck parked at the edge of the field, and a man and a woman in yellow hard hats got out. As we rode past, the woman knelt down and began hammering a wooden stake with a pink ribbon into the ground. A box filled with stakes was at her side.

"What was that about?" I asked my friends when we reached the road, my bike squeaking with every pump of my legs.

"Who knows?" Peephole called over his shoulder. "But I forgot to mention something about Mr. Babbage's yard."

"What?" Shanks and I said at the same time.

"Up in the tree right in the middle of the yard. There were some ducks up there. But I saw something else stuck in the branches."

"What?" we said again, this time less patiently.

"A fish. A *real* one."

3

Welcome to Bellwood

I never knew whether it was a coincidence or not, but the town of Bellwood was actually shaped just like a bell. And what formed most of the border of that bell? Woods! And what did we call those woods? The Bell Woods! If you were to float up in a hot-air balloon or ride in a helicopter or climb the water tower—the tallest structure in town—and look down at Bellwood, you'd think, *So* that's *why they named it that.* (Actually, it might also remind you of the shape of Darth Vader's helmet, but the town of Darthvaders-helmetwood doesn't exactly roll off the tongue.) Bellwood was widest at its south end, which was defined by Highway 43 stretching across the county in both directions. Mr. Babbage lived at the southwestern corner of the bell, right next to our headquarters.

The Bell Woods lay on top of our bell-shaped town like

a blanket. That meant that we Bellwoodians were sort of protected from the outside world. It also meant that we were isolated, which explained why we were all so weird. Actually, the One and Onlys seemed to be the only people in Bellwood who recognized and celebrated how strange the town was. (Ever notice how the people who insist that they're normal are usually the oddest ones?)

Inside the bell was our town: schools, churches, stores, houses. Honest Hardware, our family business going back for generations, was right downtown. Peephole lived in the middle of the bell, too, just a couple of blocks from Bellwood Elementary. Shanks lived up on the upper west side of town, and my house wasn't too far from hers in the upper right—northeast—corner of the bell, on Munchaus Avenue. My house was the last on the block before it dead-ended into the Bell Woods, though there was an entrance to an old forest service road that used to snake all the way through the woods but was now mostly overgrown. My backyard was fringed with the trees that formed the unofficial border of the town. At the bottom of the bell, south of Highway 43, was a lot of open space that was still technically part of Bellwood; when we were smaller, the One and Onlys used to call this area the Magical Realm of Moo-Landia. Out there? Mostly cows.

My dad liked to say, "What's the only kind of pie you don't want for dessert? A cow pie!"

I didn't know what a cow pie was, so I looked it up.

Gross, Dad.

But Moo-Landia wasn't only cows. There was also the Shamtraw estate, which was the biggest house in Bellwood because Old Man Shamtraw was the richest person in Bellwood. He had a first name, I'm sure, but nobody referred to him as anything other than Old Man Shamtraw. He lived in this huge mansion on the other side of Highway 43, and because it was pretty secluded down there, not many people knew what the house was like. There were all kinds of rumors about what Shamtraw did all alone in his mansion. One rumor said that under the estate was a series of interconnecting tunnels with hidden rooms full of priceless objects like vases from the Ming Dynasty, and that he would pass the days by tipping them off the shelves, one by one. Another rumor said that he was a vampire who had spent centuries gathering wealth while secretly sucking the blood of Bellwood's unsuspecting citizens.

My mom once told me that Old Man Shamtraw was "eccentric." I asked her what that meant, and she said it meant that he was bonkers. How come she didn't just call him bonkers? Because, she explained, he was rich. After all, he owned a lot of the land in Bellwood, including the field where the old drive-in was. I guess if you're bonkers *and* rich, you get to be *eccentric*.

Last summer, the One and Onlys spent many days across the highway, crouched in the bushes outside the Shamtraw estate, spying with binoculars to see if he really was a vampire. What can I say? We were foolish kids then, and this was the most promising mystery Bellwood had to offer. Of course, we didn't see any vampiric activity, but we did see a lot of yard-maintenance workers. Finally, after a week or so, Shamtraw himself came out and asked us what the heck we found so interesting about his front gate. We didn't have a good answer for him, but we did learn an important lesson: if we were going to be world-class detectives, we needed to hone our covert-surveillance skills. He politely told us to buzz off, and when he skulked back to his mansion, he gave the impression of a ghost who was annoyed that he still had to do all that haunting.

You couldn't blame us for investigating. Like I said, we knew that Bellwood was brimming with strange things—you just had to know where to look.

Like the annual Bellwood Bratwurst Bonanza. The Triple B was a cooking competition in July that everybody looked forward to each year. The challenge was to make an original dish that featured the German sausage as the centerpiece. Why bratwurst? Well, that's a story that goes way back in the history of our town. Legend has it that one of the early mayors of Bellwood, a German-American fellow named Wolfgang Munchaus, was nuts about pigs. And by that I mean that he liked to eat them. A lot. It was said that Munchaus raised a whole farm of pigs so that he would always have plenty of bacon, ham, pork, sausage, jowl, hock, spare ribs, and, of course, bratwurst to eat.

As the story goes, Bellwood fell on hard times. The road that used to pass through town was moved, and so visitors stopped visiting, passersby stopped passing by, and shoppers stopped shopping. Munchaus found himself in danger of becoming the mayor of a ghost town. So he came up with a brilliant idea: he would throw a huge festival that would attract visitors far and wide. And the main event at the festival would be—you guessed it—a bratwurst contest!

Munchaus's plan worked. The festival was a huge success. Munchaus himself judged the bratwurst contest and, in a slightly controversial decision, awarded his own recipes first place, second place, and third place. It was a good day for Mayor Munchaus, and for Bellwood. The Bonanza continued to draw crowds year after year, and eventually people started moving to Bellwood, and the town found itself back on its feet. Over the decades, some of the guidelines had changed (now, for instance, you could enter other sausages into the cook-off), but the spirit of togetherness and celebration remained.

If you won the Triple B, you earned the respect and admiration of the entire town. And you got a trophy of a little golden (plastic) bratwurst. Oh, and a T-shirt that said I'M THE WIENER! I always thought the T-shirt was like something you should have to wear if you lost.

My parents, along with pretty much everybody else in Bellwood, had always entered the Triple B, but they never won it. Mr. Babbage, whose yard had been invaded by ducks, was the undisputed champion of the bratwurst cook-off, the LeBron James of German sausage, the Napoleon of encased meats. He'd won it the last five years in a row, and it was generally agreed that his bratwurst dishes were things of unparalleled beauty. The judges, who were members of the town council, always maintained that it was anybody's Bonanza, that any competitor could win first place, but the moment you saw their faces when they tasted Babbage's entry, you knew they were going to send him through to the final round—at which point it was up to the chief taster, Mr. Pocus, to choose the winner. Even that old grump couldn't deny that Babbage's sausages were divine.

I'm actually not crazy about bratwurst, which makes me unusual in Bellwood. The year that my parents won second place—bested only by Mr. Babbage's Brat & Cabbages—we ate tater brats (fried potato and bratwurst) for a week. Finally, I made the mistake of complaining.

"This isn't bad," my dad said. "It's the *wurst.*"

This year my parents had something special up their sleeves. I entered the kitchen to find them both hunched over the stove, inspecting the contents of a frying pan. The kitchen smelled like maple syrup.

My mom was chewing on her thumbnail and squinting with deep concentration. My dad tugged at the hairs of his beard, which hugged his face like the chinstrap of a football helmet. I was never sure why my dad didn't grow a mustache, too. Whenever anybody asked about his mustacheless beard, he'd reply, "If it was good enough for Honest Abe Lincoln, then it's good enough for me."

How can you argue with that?

"What's up?" I said, and they both jumped.

"Paul!" My mom clutched at her throat. "We're deep in experimentation here. I really think we're onto something."

"I'm glad you're home," my dad said. "I need you to do something for us." Lately, it seemed like my dad was only ever in one of two places: the kitchen or the family store. Honest Hardware wasn't a big place—just an open room with some aisles of tools, lawn-care stuff, household items, nuts and bolts—but it had everything most Bellwood residents needed. Like I said, it was a family business: his dad worked there before him, and his dad's dad had established the store. It was probably expected that I'd take it over someday, but we never really talked much about that.

A few days earlier, I overheard my parents whispering to each other in the kitchen. I could tell they were talking about the store, and they sounded worried. I could have sworn I heard them repeat the same word over and over again: *conquistador.* When I came in, they changed the subject immediately. I wondered what it could mean.

"A job for me? What is it?" I asked, a little concerned about the answer.

"Clear a space on the mantelpiece. Make it big enough for a trophy."

"*Jerry,*" my mom said. "Don't get cocky."

I was intrigued. "So what's the plan this year?"

"Everybody likes pancakes, right?" my mom asked.

"Sure."

"And everybody likes bratwurst."

"Well . . ."

"So we figured we'd put them together!" She was clearly very excited about this idea.

I wanted to be on board, but I wasn't convinced yet.

My dad ignored my hesitation. "You've heard of pigs in a blanket, right? Well, say hello to the future Triple B first-prize dish: Swine in a Sleeping Bag."

They both beamed at me with big, toothy grins, obviously expecting some kind of reaction.

"I'll go clear off the mantelpiece."

"Atta boy!" my dad yelled, then high-fived my mom.

The sound of screeching tires woke me from a deep sleep in the middle of the night. I sat bolt upright in my bed, caught in that startled, foggy space between my dreams and the darkness of my room. Had I dreamed the sound?

But then I could hear the hum of a car engine speeding by my house.

The clock on my dresser read 12:43 a.m. I swiveled out of bed and stumbled clumsily to the window that overlooked the road. With a little effort, I creaked it open and thrust my head out into the night air, but there was no sign of a car on Munchaus Avenue. I looked to my right in time to see a pair of red taillights disappearing into the entrance to the old overgrown forest road. The lights bounced and jostled, and then the hulking trees of the Bell Woods, outlined in black in the night, enveloped them. And just like that, the stillness of the night returned.

I tried to remember the last time I'd seen a car drive down that old dirt road. It'd been a long time. I watched the mouth of the road for a minute or two, wondering maybe if the car would come back out once the driver realized that nature had reclaimed the path up ahead, but there was no sign of it. Right as I was about to go back to bed, a small noise from across the street caught my attention. There, gliding from the Wagners' garage, across the front lawn, and up to their front steps was a dark figure. I squinted to get a better look. By the dull shine of the porch light, I watched as Janice Wagner, my old babysitter, silently opened her front door, cast a sharp glance down the street, and then disappeared into the house. What was she up to, sneaking around at this hour? And had she heard the screeching of the tires, too?

I listened to the night for a moment longer, but there was only the soft chorus of insects and a slight breeze rustling through the trees. I was struck by the feeling that something was about to happen in Bellwood. Or maybe it had already begun happening. What was coming to our little town? And what did the duckies on Babbage's lawn, their little yellow bodies floating atop his grass, have to do with it? Were they some kind of message of things to come? Or were they a warning?

And then the feeling passed, and I was tired again. The urge to sleep was already overtaking me, and I yawned, rubbed my eyes, and slunk back to the comfort of my bed.

Man vs. Lawn

It was Wednesday, and that meant it was time for another round of Paul vs. the Lawn. It wasn't a fair fight. The lawn was big and wide, with thousands of blades of grass. All I had was an old rusty push mower that we'd owned since way before I was born, maybe before the dawn of humankind. We *did* have a beautiful, gleaming GrassMaster 3000 riding mower in the garage, but my dad wouldn't let me use it. He called it the "Cadillac of lawn-maintenance devices" and said that I needed to foster a *respect for the lawn* before I could fire it up. What did that even mean?

I wasn't exactly thrilled about the job, but I didn't have a choice. My dad expected it to be mowed by the time he got home from the hardware store, and when it came to the lawn, you couldn't really reason with him. Besides, a little "me-time" to contemplate the mystery of the duckies while I mowed the lawn was just what I needed. In fact, "me-time" was the only kind of time available, because my mom was out running errands. Leaving me alone at the house was a new thing, and my parents still seemed a little uncomfortable with it, but they said that I was getting old enough to take care of myself. I liked the way that sounded: taking care of myself. But something about it also made me a little nervous. What if the house caught on fire? What if Ronald ate another action figure? What if *I* accidentally ate an action figure . . . and then set the house on fire?

The mower clanged and wheezed like some medieval torture device as I pushed it through the grass. The dry grass. Of course it was dry: Bellwood, and the whole region, was in the middle of a drought. That's why the forest fires outside of town were so hard to contain. Mrs. Willis, the chief of the Bellwood Fire Department, and Byron, her teenage son, a Junior Firefighter, had visited our class at the end of the school year and talked about some of the ways they were helping to fight the fires. I think Peephole paid particularly close attention because he was transfixed by Byron, who also had loose, stringy limbs and must have been the tallest kid in high school. If Bellwood had a contest to see who was the lankiest, those two would be the favorites.

At the time, the forest fires didn't feel real to me. But now it was kind of scary to think that we were going about our lives, business as usual, while the woods not too far down the road were on fire. The helicopters buzzing by over our heads, going to and from the fires, were getting to be a normal thing, and they were a constant reminder that a strong change in the wind was all it would take for the wildfires to come toward Bellwood, like a monster banging on our walls, wanting to be let in.

So why *was* Babbage's grass wet? Even if he had watered it with a hose or a sprinkler, that didn't account for the ducks, or the fish in the tree. I had a hunch that the water, the ducks, and the fish all came from the same place, and that Babbage had nothing to do with it. But where?

Shanks mentioned that the ducks could have come from the sewer, and there was the interesting fact of the manhole cover in the yard. But that didn't explain the fish and random ducks in the tree. *Mister E*, I thought, *where did you come from?*

I was only about a quarter of the way through mowing the lawn, and already my arms were starting to feel like wet ropes. I had an urge to ride my bike to the hardware store and yell, "You know what I respect? *The lawn!* What a great lawn! What a green lawn! What a respectable lawn!" But my dad would never fall for that. "Finish the job," he'd say. And then he'd probably add another item to my list of things to do.

I caught a glimpse of my dog, Ronald, staring at me from the window. I thought I detected pity in his eyes. Ronald . . . now there was a reasonable guy. He was an old boxer with a droopy white face like melting vanilla ice cream. He only ever moved when it was time to eat, and even then he preferred to have his meals delivered directly to his face. Aside from the action-figure incident and one or two poor decisions involving certain bodily functions and the living room rug, he was probably the most level-headed member of the Marconi household. If I told him about the ducks, he wouldn't be surprised at all.

Ronald's ears pricked up and his head tilted to the side. I whirled around and saw a chubby squirrel snacking on an acorn in the tree directly behind me. *At least you* belong *in a tree*, I thought, *not like that fish*. The fish, the fish. If only we knew where it came from. . . . An idea hit me; I knew what we needed to do!

I pulled out my phone and dashed off a text to Peephole and Shanks.

Calling the One and Onlys! Meet at HQ in 30. We need to snag the fish in the tree!

I stopped pushing the mower—I'd finish this job later in the day—and turned for the house, already formulating a plan in my head. My phone chimed with a text. Shanks replied with an emoji of a fish. Peephole sent a smiley face, and maybe it was just me, but it looked a little nauseous.

→ 5 ←

Operation Stinky Fish

"The fish could be the key to the whole mystery," I said to Peephole and Shanks. The three of us were hunkered down at our headquarters at the edge of the Bell Woods. "Remember that day in science class when we learned about ecosystems, and how every animal exists in an environment that supports it?"

Shanks nodded, but Peephole was staring uneasily at the overgrown field, mentally preparing himself for coming face to face with a dead fish. I knew he was very concerned about the bacteria that a decaying fish might have, because he was wearing safety goggles that were too big for his face and bulky winter gloves. He looked like a deep-sea diver at the North Pole.

"So that means that if we can identify what kind of fish it is, then we can maybe figure out where it came from. And if we can figure out where the fish is from, then we'll know where the ducks are from."

"On a scale of one to barf, how stinky do you think a dead fish is?" Peephole asked gravely.

"I'm not sure," I said, "but probably closer to barf."

"You don't have to worry about that," Shanks said, "because only one of us needs to get the fish. And since I'm the best tree climber, that'll be me."

"So that leaves Paul and me on lookout?" Peephole asked hopefully.

"Not lookout. Distraction. I can't just waltz into Babbage's backyard and climb his tree. He'll see me. He'll come out. He'll want to know what I'm doing. Your job is to distract him."

"How are we supposed to do that?" Peephole asked.

"We'll knock on his door," I suggested. "When he answers, we'll talk to him."

"About what? The weather? 'Gee, hi, Mr. Babbage. Say, how about this wacky weather we're having? I can't remember the last time it rained ducks.'"

"How about this? We're going door to door and asking if anyone's seen your lost cat."

Peephole thought about this. "Not bad. It could work. What color is it?"

"The cat? Uh, how about black?"

"Paul, I would never have a black cat. I'm scared of them."

"Well, then, it's orange."

"An orange cat? What is this, a Dr. Seuss book?"

Shanks interrupted impatiently. "Your cat is a fluffy white Persian with a fluorescent green collar that has a little bell attached to it. His name is Mel, but he only answers to 'Kitty' and he likes bacon and snuggling and standing in front of the television when reruns of *Sponge-Bob SquarePants* are on. He's your best friend and you love him and you just want to know if Mr. Babbage has seen him."

Peephole squinted, filing it all away in his photographic memory, and gave a swift bob of his head. "Got it."

We rode our bikes to Babbage's house. Peephole and I dismounted and marched directly up the front walk to Mr. Babbage's door. Shanks splintered off to the side of the house, according to our plan. When she was in position behind a big bush, she flashed us a thumbs-up.

"Let me do the talking," I whispered. "Maybe we can find out more about the ducks." I reached up to press the doorbell, but before I could, the door swung open and Mr. Babbage, again in his red silk bathrobe, frowned down at us.

"Yes?" he grunted.

Peephole and I stared up at him, struck by his appearance. His thin black hair, which was usually so carefully combed to the side, was poking out in all directions. His eyes had a weary look, like he hadn't slept a wink since the duckies showed up. Odd music drifted out from inside the house, a choir of voices whose singing was interrupted occasionally by sharp whoops and hollers, as if one by one the choir members were having ice-cold water dumped on their heads.

"Hello, Mr. Babbage," Peephole blurted, surprising me so much that I glanced over at him. He was still wearing the safety goggles and winter gloves. "We're knocking on your door because my cat, SpongeBob, has lost his bacon and I'm wondering if you've seen it."

I winced, trying to maintain a friendly smile.

"No, I mean . . . my cat's name is Mel, not SpongeBob. He likes to watch *SpongeBob*, but he doesn't really understand what's going on. I mean, that's not important. . . ."

"Son," Mr. Babbage broke in, "why are you wearing goggles and gloves?"

"Oh, these?" Peephole's voice wavered. "These are safety precautions. You see, my cat is very dangerous. He likes to bite hands and faces. He's an orange cat who likes to . . . no . . . he's a white cat. . . . Well, he used to be orange, but now he's white and . . ."

Without moving my head, I looked over to where Shanks was hiding. No sign of her, which meant she was already in the backyard, retrieving the fish.

"What my friend means to say," I cut in, hoping to save the visit before Babbage slammed the door on us, "is that he's lost his cat. It's white. It's fluffy. Have you seen it?"

Babbage shifted his eyes to me, and he seemed grateful

that I had said something that made sense. The voices behind him droned and then whooped, droned and then whooped. The whoops were getting higher-pitched, so maybe the water was getting colder.

Babbage noted the confusion on my face. "My music," he said, fumbling in his bathrobe pocket for a small remote, which he pressed. The music stopped. "I know it's loud, but it's therapeutic. It helps us relax." He ran a delicate finger across the bridge of his nose. "I'm sorry, kids, but we haven't seen anything all day. But, then, we haven't been outside, either."

"We?" I asked.

"Calvin Coolidge and me." Mr. Babbage creaked the door open enough for us to see into the living room, where his little white dog was curled on the sofa, its face half buried in its paws. "Cal and I have been a little on edge today. Haven't we, Cal?"

Cal let out a growly flutter of a response, then turned away.

"Because of the ducks?" I asked.

Babbage's and Cal's faces snapped quickly to me, startled.

"I saw them yesterday morning," I continued. "We all did. I mean"—I caught myself, gesturing over to Peephole—"we both did."

The mere mention of the duckies seemed to make Babbage stiffen with fear. He slowly reached a finger into his mouth and bit down on the nail, shifting his tense gaze between Peephole and me. "Yes, well," he said finally, "it was quite the spectacle, wasn't it? It may have been a bundle of fun for the neighborhood, but it's been heck on wheels for Calvin and me." He shot a sympathetic glance to Calvin Coolidge on the sofa, who returned the same look to his master. "You see, Cal and I, we're a couple of nervous Nellies. And we don't appreciate uninvited visitors."

I withered a little at the obvious jab, but Peephole didn't seem to notice. "I understand completely," he said, with genuine concern in his voice. "Do the police have any leads on the case?"

Babbage let out a joyless chirp of a laugh. "The police aren't the least bit concerned with it. Apparently, there are more important things happening in Bellwood, though I can't imagine what." He waved his hand dismissively. "But it doesn't matter. I know exactly who put the ducks in my yard."

"You do?" I said, glancing at Peephole in excitement, but he was staring at the bush at the side of the house, where Shanks had reappeared, dangling a zip-up plastic bag with the fish in it. Shanks was grinning widely, swishing the bag back and forth with a nauseating wet slap of a noise. Peephole's eyes followed the fish like it was a hypnotist's gold watch. I elbowed him, but he wouldn't snap out of it.

"What is it?" Babbage asked, poking his head out the

front door just as Shanks ducked back out of sight behind the bush.

"Nothing!" I spat out. "We thought we saw Mel the cat, but it was just a . . . uh . . . bush. Anyway, you were saying that you think you know who is responsible for the duckies?"

Babbage stepped back into the house and grimaced. "Pocus—my neighbor." He almost coughed the words, jerking a thumb to indicate the house to his right. At the sound of the name, Calvin Coolidge ripped out a mean little bark. Peephole did, too. "Why they allow that little monster around children I'll never understand."

"You're telling *me*," Peephole said.

"You're saying Mr. Pocus put the ducks in your yard? Why would he do that?" I asked.

"Head games, my young friends," Babbage replied, tapping his forehead with his index finger. "He's trying to rattle us before the Triple B this weekend. He knows that we're preparing our secret recipe, and he'll do anything to sabotage our work. Because that man has always had it out for us, hasn't he, Cal?"

Cal groaned in agreement.

"You see, the only thing he cares about are his tomato plants. He spends all spring and summer in his backyard, swooning over them. He clips them, he waters them, he even sings to them."

Peephole nodded enthusiastically. "Most teachers have

a framed picture of their families, or maybe Abraham Lincoln, on their desks. Mr. Pocus had a photo of a tomato."

"If you ask me, it's downright bizarre," Babbage continued. "A few years ago, he got it into his head that Cal was going over there and . . . and . . . *relieving* himself on his tomatoes, if you catch my meaning. He had the audacity to accuse my best friend of such an undignified act." I looked over at Calvin Coolidge, and it may have just been me, but I thought he was looking a little guilty. "I told Pocus in no uncertain terms that he was dead wrong. And then you know what he said? He said maybe it was *me* who had soiled his tomatoes. Well, that was about all I could handle, and the two of us got into a shouting match. Quite a sight for the neighbors, I'm sure. Shortly after that, Pocus built that ridiculous fence between our yards, and we haven't spoken since. You know what? I'm glad the barrier is there. I don't even want to see his silly tomatoes."

"Wow," I said, shaking my head in disbelief. "That's quite a feud between you two. But Pocus is the chief taster in the Triple B. If he wanted to sabotage your chances, couldn't he just give the trophy to someone else?"

Babbage dismissed my question with a curt shake of his head. "Some things are sacred, my young friends. As loathsome as Pocus is, he has too much respect for the Triple B to crown a false winner. In fact, the year before I entered for the first time, Pocus declared that none of the entries were worthy of winning the trophy." It was true. My parents still talked about the year the Triple B had no wiener winner. They used it as motivation to make their recipes "Pocus-worthy."

"The truth is," Babbage continued, "Pocus knows that my sausages are simply the best." An obvious hint of pride came into his voice when he talked about the Triple B. After all, he was the reigning champion of the last five Bonanzas, which made him a celebrity in our town. And that right there tells you a lot about Bellwood. "It kills him every year to do it, yet he has no choice but to declare me the winner."

I guess some things are more important than rivalries. And bratwurst is one of them.

"Why the ducks?" Peephole asked. "What does it mean?"

Babbage tossed his hands up. "I admit, I'm a bit puzzled by that. When they first appeared, I didn't know what to make of them at all. But the more I think about it, the more certain I am that Pocus is behind it. He knows that Cal and I are delicate creatures and that we don't handle stress well. It's a perfect crime, if you think about it, because it's *not* a crime. Nobody would suspect him, and if they did, what could they do about it? All he wants to do is declare me the loser of the Triple B, but he knows he can't do that unless my bratwurst is not up to snuff." He narrowed his eyes, and his expression took on a more determined edge. "He's made a big mistake if he thinks he can get away with this. You know what Sir Isaac Newton said. . . ."

I bit my lip and tried to remember our science lesson on Isaac Newton. Science was after lunch, so sometimes I was a little sleepy.

"Ouch! Who threw this apple at me?" Peephole said, chuckling, but Babbage didn't crack a smile.

It came to me: "For every action, there is an equal and opposite reaction."

"That's right," Babbage said, pointing at me. "What goes around comes around."

Just then a helicopter thundered by overhead. Peephole covered his ears against the noise.

Babbage's face soured, and he muttered something that got lost in all the roaring.

"What was that?" I asked when the helicopter had passed.

Babbage sniffed twice. "Do I smell fish?"

Shanks had been edging closer to the front door to hear Babbage's story, but now she darted back behind the bush with the tree fish.

"Oh, uh, that's us," I said. "We were looking for the cat in the garbage. . . . Well, speaking of Mel, we'd better keep looking for him!" I grabbed Peephole by the arm and wheeled around, and together we bounded down the front walk. "Thanks for the chat, Mr. Babbage!" I called over my shoulder. "And thanks to Cal, too!"

I could hear the ice-water choir crank up again as we hopped on our bikes and pedaled back toward our head-quarters. Meanwhile, Shanks had cut through Babbage's yard and looped around his house; she met us in the road just as a police car cruised past us, going the opposite direction. Officer Portnoy was in the driver's seat, and though I gave him a quick wave, he kept his eyes focused on the road ahead of him. Safety comes first.

The One and Onlys were buzzing with energy, loaded with fresh leads and a real piece of evidence, which was swinging back and forth from Shanks's handlebars in its slimy plastic bag.

"We're going to crack this case soon!" Shanks hollered. "I can taste it."

"And I can smell it," Peephole whined, steering his bike uneasily with one gloved hand while the other plugged his nose.

6

Fishing for Answers

Back at our headquarters, we sat in a circle under the lean-to, the bagged fish resting in front of us like a Ouija board. Even through the plastic bag, its pungent stench wafted up to our noses.

"I'm never having sushi again," I said.

"That's good," Peephole replied. "Consuming raw fish is a great way to pick up a variety of food-borne illnesses."

"So . . . what do we do with it?" Shanks asked.

I shrugged. "I don't know. Maybe we should name it."

"Name the fish? But it's dead," Peephole said.

"It's dead *now*," I replied. "It wasn't always dead. If you got a fish from the pet store, you'd have to name it, wouldn't you?"

Peephole cocked his head. "Not necessarily. You have to name dogs and cats. Fish are a gray area."

"Well, I feel bad for it," I said. "This poor fish was probably just doing normal fish things, hanging out with fish friends, living its fish life, when all of a sudden—*whammo!*—something happened, and it ended up hanging upside down from a tree in Babbage's backyard."

"How about 'Tina Fish'?" Shanks suggested.

"She looks like a Tina," I agreed. "So where did you come from, Tina Fish? And how come you ended up in Babbage's tree?"

"Babbage sounds pretty sure Mr. Pocus is behind this," Shanks said. "And the two of them definitely have bad blood. But . . ."

"You're not convinced it was Mr. Pocus, are you?" I asked.

"Nope," she confirmed. "The duckies . . . they're too . . . *weird*. If Mr. Pocus wanted to get even with Babbage for what he thought he did to his tomatoes, there are so many ways to do it. Ways that make a lot more sense."

"Don't underestimate Mr. Pocus's ability to be evil," Peephole said bitterly, "even if it's a weird kind of evil. I bet it was him."

I could see in his eyes the entire year of grief Mr. Pocus had given him. That kind of torment doesn't just go away. "Should we do surveillance on his house?" I asked.

Shanks shook her head. "Remember how well that worked out with Old Man Shamtraw last summer? And Pocus would probably do a lot worse than simply tell us to get lost."

"So do we knock on his door and ask him about it?" I suggested.

"Not me." Shanks crossed her arms. "That guy will turn you to stone just by looking at you."

"I think you know my stance on talking with Mr. Pocus," Peephole said firmly. "I'd rather eat a bowl of slug chili . . ."

"I guess I'm not up for it, either," I admitted.

But Peephole wasn't finished. ". . . slug chili that's been left out overnight in the rain, and a family of raccoons has been nibbling at it, and a cat with the flu has hacked up a fur ball in it, and—"

"I think 'slug chili' was enough to get your point across, Peephole," Shanks said.

"No, it wasn't," Peephole continued with a full head of steam. "Slug chili that's been found by a rabid woodpecker and been used as a . . . a—"

"How about we focus on Tina?" I suggested, cutting him off before he worked himself up too much. "What do we know about her?"

"So far?" Shanks said. "She's very smelly and very dead."

We studied Tina for a while in perplexed silence. She wasn't a particularly large or small fish—much bigger than a goldfish but not big enough to take your picture with her. She was just about the size of one of my dad's shoes, and smelled only slightly worse. She had a fin on her back and a red belly, unlike her more yellow and orange back and side. All over her body was a crazy pattern of squiggly lines, like a tiger. Her mouth hung open and her eyes bulged out, like she had just been told something shocking.

What's your secret? I wondered.

Peephole whipped out his phone and tapped at the screen with his thumbs. "I'm doing a quick search for 'types of fish.'" His thumbs stopped moving, and he read the screen. "There are 187,000,000 results. We need to be more specific."

I guessed that the odds of Tina coming from the ocean, where the water was salty, were slim. Bellwood was nowhere near any ocean, but there were plenty of lakes and rivers around, and I remembered a lesson in science class about lakes having freshwater. "Try 'types of freshwater fish,'" I suggested, and leaned in to see the results. Peephole tapped on a picture of a diagram of the most common types of freshwater fish. There were hundreds of them.

"Ugh," Shanks said, her face contorted in frustration. "This isn't working."

"We could be here all day," Peephole sighed. "Where's a fish expert when you need one?"

"That's it!" I yelled, startling my friends. If Tina were alive, she would have been startled, too. "I happen to know a fish expert. And we can go talk to her right now. C'mon." I hustled out of the lean-to. "Let's ride to my dad's store."

When we entered Honest Hardware, my dad was down on his hands and knees in the adhesives aisle, helping a customer gather up a spill. He looked up and gave us all a quick wave, but the customer, who I realized was Darrel Sullivan, the guy with the goatee, kept his eyes on the roll of red duct tape that he was scrambling after.

Bella Tuff was where she always was on Wednesdays: in the back room, hunched over a keyboard, typing numbers into a spreadsheet. For years she'd been coming in twice a week, on Tuesdays and Wednesdays, to help my dad keep his inventory records up to date. Bella was a funny lady; she was a little loud and a little rough, but if she liked you, she'd treat you like royalty. And, more important, she was a lifelong fisherwoman. Not only had she fished all around the state, but she was always taking trips to fish in other parts of the world. If anybody was going to know what kind of fish Tina was, it would be Bella Tuff.

The One and Onlys crowded in the doorway to the back office. Bella's broad back was to us, and all we could see was a small explosion of brown curly hair with streaks of silver just inches away from the computer screen.

I tapped softly on the door frame. She didn't move.

"Bella?" I said, and at the sound of her name the swift pop of her fingers against the keyboard stopped. Still, she didn't turn around.

Peephole and Shanks shot me questioning glances, and I made a reassuring gesture. "Bella, it's me."

With effort, she swiveled around, flashing a scowl at the interruption. But when she saw us, her face broke into a wide, tooth-showing smile. "Ah, Paul," she cooed in her deep, melodious voice. "And your friends . . . Don't tell me . . . Shark and Pea Pod. Hey, how come you don't have a funny nickname, Paul?"

"Unlucky, I guess."

Shanks smiled. "Nice to see you, Ms. Tuff."

"Call me Bella, darling. What can I do for you kids?" As soon as the question was out of her mouth, her smile faded. She sniffed the air once. Twice. She looked us up and down with wary eyes. Tina had made her presence known. "Unless you all came to ask advice on personal hygiene, I think I smell a fish. And not a fresh one."

I held up the plastic bag with Tina in it. "That's why we came to see you. We've got a little mystery on our hands, and we thought you could help us. You know everything there is to know about fish, right?"

Bella blushed and gave a modest shake of her head, but the smile on her face said, *Yes. I do know everything there is to know about fish.*

"See, we've got this fish." I jiggled the plastic bag, which was not a good idea because it sent tiny waves of fish stink into the air. "But we don't know what kind of fish it is. And we were hoping you could identify it."

As politely as she could, Bella plugged her nose with her thumb and forefinger, then rolled her chair closer to the bag, squinting. "Paul . . . ," she began. "How long have you been carrying around this dead fish?"

"Just this morning," I answered.

"And I'm sure there's a good reason why you're hanging on to it?"

"It's evidence."

She stared at me.

"It's kind of a long story, Bella."

"I see. You catch it up at Schuylerville Lake?"

"Her," Peephole said.

"Huh?"

"Tina," Shanks explained, pointing at Tina.

"Oh. Did you catch *Tina* up at Schuylerville Lake?"

"We found her, actually," I said.

"Found her where?"

"In a tree," Peephole said.

Bella studied Peephole for a moment. "A wise guy, huh?"

"He's not kidding," I said quickly. "We found her in a tree in Mr. Babbage's backyard. You know—the bratwurst guy?"

Bella's face changed slightly, and her body stiffened a little. "Yes, I know Lance. You found this fish in his backyard?"

"Along with a small army of rubber duckies," Peephole added. "I'm surprised you didn't hear about it. It's the only cool thing that's happened in Bellwood so far this summer."

Bella frowned a moment, and her eyebrows twisted with uncertainty. For a second, she was lost in thought.

Then, quickly, she sat up straight and folded her fingers together. "I was sick in bed all day yesterday. Didn't even come to work." Her voice was flat and definite.

"Why did you ask if we'd been fishing at Schuylerville Lake?" Shanks asked.

Bella's shoulders seemed to relax a little. "Because your fish, it's—uh, *she*—is a tiger trout. You can tell by the stripes. In fact, I've got a few of her friends in my freezer. See, I'm working on a 'troutwurst' dish for this weekend's Triple B. It's a little unusual, but I think it might turn some heads. I've always been overlooked by the judges, but this year is going to be different." She clenched her jaw, and I could see how determined she was. It looked like my parents weren't the only ones stepping up their game. "Anyway," she continued, "our little friend here definitely made her home in Schuylerville Lake."

"How can you be so sure?" Shanks asked.

"Because tiger trout aren't native to these parts, so you have to ship them in. I have some friends who work in the state department of fish and wildlife, and I happen to know that last spring there was a problem with fish overpopulation in Schuylerville Lake. So they stocked the lake with a bunch of tiger trout. See, tiger trout eat other fish, and they're sterile, which means they don't reproduce. So if you want to cut down a population of fish that's gotten out of control, just add a bunch of tiger trout."

"Cool," Shanks said.

"So Tina was a cannibal?" Peephole asked.

Bella chuckled. "I guess you could say that."

"You really are a fish expert, huh?" Peephole said. "Can I ask you a question?"

Bella grinned. "Shoot."

"How much fish poop do you suppose is in a mouthful of lake water?"

"Eh?"

"I mean, like, a little bit of fish poop? Or are we talking a lot of fish poop?"

"Brilliant question," Shanks said, annoyed. "You're really helping us crack this case wide open, Peephole."

"Sorry," he said defensively. "But it's all I can think about. Three summers ago, my parents took me swimming at Schuylerville Lake. I brought a bucket to make sand castles with, but instead I filled it up with lake water and drank it all."

Shanks and I made a disgusted face. Even Bella seemed to grimace.

"I was thirsty! I didn't know I couldn't drink it! Later that day I got real sick, but my parents couldn't figure out why. They even took me to the doctor. I puked all over the waiting room."

"What did the doctor say?" I asked.

"He said, 'Don't worry, my receptionist will clean that up.'"

"No, I mean about why you were sick!"

"Oh. When he found out we had been at the lake, he

asked if I accidentally drank any of the water. I told him no, I drank it on purpose."

"Well, Pea Pod, it sounds like you learned something from that experience." Still facing us, Bella rolled herself back to the desk. "Now, if you'll notice, this room that we're in doesn't have any windows, which means that Tina— or her stench, that is—will be lingering in the air long after you guys leave. So, if there's nothing else I can help you kids with, I'm going to finish up with my work and then pay a visit to aisle four: air fresheners."

With that, she spun slowly on her chair, leaning in toward her computer screen again and commencing the *click click pop* of the keyboard.

Shanks and I turned to go, but Peephole stood frozen, his eyes fixed on Bella's desk.

"What'd you have?" he asked, his voice a little too loud.

Bella stopped typing but didn't turn around. "Huh?"

"You said you were sick yesterday. What'd you have?"

Bella spun around to face us again, but there was a wary look on her face. "Flu."

"You don't look sick to me," Peephole said.

"Dude!" I whisper-yelled under my breath. I didn't know what had come over him, but Bella was a family friend.

"Twenty-four-hour bug, I guess," Bella said flatly.

Peephole crossed his arms. "Are you sure you were in bed all day yesterday?"

"I'm positive," Bella shot back. She shifted her gaze to

me. "Paul, I'm fairly certain your friend isn't a doctor, so is there a reason he's so concerned with my health?"

I blushed. "Uh . . . Peephole wants everybody to take care of themselves—right, Peephole?" I threw a sharp look in his direction, but he was still staring at Bella's desk. I followed his eyes and finally saw the reason for his weird behavior.

On the desk, next to a framed picture of Bella holding a massive fish in her arms, was a little yellow rubber ducky. It looked identical to the ducks in Babbage's yard.

"Well, I appreciate the goodwill," Bella said sarcastically, "but I've got to get back to work." She spun around again, sighed deeply, shook her head of curls, and settled into a steady *click click pop.*

$\Rightarrow$ 7 $\Leftarrow$

Just a Friendly Chat

We kneeled down and used our hands and some sticks to dig a small grave about thirty paces from our headquarters, which we figured was far enough away so that we wouldn't be smelling Tina Fish every time we went there. Her funeral should have been a simple, solemn affair, but I was distracted by the ducky I had seen in Bella's office.

"If there's a heaven for fish," I said, tossing dirt over Tina, "I know that's where you are now."

"Even though you were a cannibal," Peephole added. Shanks gave him a small punch on the arm. He mouthed "Ouch," then said, "I don't trust her."

"But she's dead," I said.

"Not Tina. Bella Tuff. She was lying about being sick."

"You're just upset she called you Pea Pod," I said, though

I couldn't ignore the ducky on her desk. I'd known Bella forever, but Peephole was right . . . in this case, at least. Bella was acting . . . well . . . *fishy.* "You didn't mention seeing her at Babbage's yesterday, and your photographic memory is never wrong."

The pride my compliment elicited was clear on Peephole's face. "Even still, that doesn't mean she wasn't there before or after us. And besides, if she *wasn't* at Babbage's, then that means she got the ducky from somewhere else. And that's more suspicious."

"B-b-but . . . ," I sputtered, desperate to come up with a reason to let Bella off the hook. "Why would she do that to Babbage? She has no motive!"

"Of course she does," Peephole shot back. "She said it herself: she wants to win the Triple B, and obviously Babbage is her biggest competition. And did you see how weird she got when we mentioned Babbage? It's like the two have history."

I scoffed, but again Peephole was right. Bella *did* get weird when we said Babbage's name. "She wants to win the Triple B, so she puts a bunch of rubber duckies in the Bratwurst King's yard? What kind of sense does that make?"

Peephole tapped his nose. "She's hiding something, dude," he said with absolute confidence. "I'd bet my life on it."

"Whatever," I said, because it was the only thing that

came to mind. "I bet she's right about Tina coming from Schuylerville Lake, though. And maybe that means the duckies came from there, too."

"Why would a bunch of rubber duckies be floating in Schuylerville Lake?" Peephole asked.

"Why would they be in Babbage's yard?" I countered. "The whole thing doesn't make sense!"

"Guys!" Shanks hissed. "We're in the middle of a funeral. Show some respect!"

"Oh, yeah," Peephole said. "Sorry."

We stood in silence, staring down at the little mound of fresh dirt.

"Swim on, Tina," Shanks finally whispered, her hand on her heart. "Swim on."

A noise startled us. It was a low, deep gurgle, like a wet belch.

"Tina? Is that you?" Peephole said, staring at the mound of dirt.

"It came from over there," Shanks whispered, "by our headquarters."

Bleeyurp.

"There it is again!"

We raced toward the noise, with Shanks easily bolting ahead of Peephole and me. When we caught up to her, we saw the source of the noise standing next to our lean-to, holding Mister E in his hand.

"Hello, kids," Officer Portnoy said slowly, never taking

his eyes off Mister E. "I hope you don't mind me dropping by your little secret hideout."

The three of us stood silently, unsure of what to make of Officer Portnoy's presence. He was the first person other than the One and Onlys to visit our headquarters.

"I see you've got a ducky here. That's interesting." He shifted his eyes from the ducky to us, looking us over one at a time. "And I see you've got dirt on your hands and knees. Been doing some digging? That's also—*brrrup*—interesting."

I swallowed hard. There was something in his voice I didn't like, and it wasn't just the belching. He seemed cautious and measured, like he'd caught us in the middle of committing a crime.

"Do you need our help with a case?" I said hopefully.

Portnoy carefully straightened his hat. "Two cases, as it turns out. You see, I was just over at Mr. Pocus's house. Somebody has torn up his tomato garden, and he's very upset. Destruction of property is a serious crime, kids. Did you know that? Well, Mr. Pocus had his suspicions about who was responsible, and so I interviewed a . . . ahem . . . neighbor of his. And this neighbor told me that some strange kids had been around there, pretending to look for a lost cat. And then it hit me: Didn't I see Macaroni and his two friends riding their bikes into these woods, fleeing the scene of the crime?"

"We didn't tear up any tomato bushes!" Shanks interjected. "It was probably Calvin Coolidge!"

Portnoy blinked. "The president?"

"The terrier," I said.

Portnoy waved the whole interruption away. "So I followed your trail back here, found your little lair, and discovered our friend here." He turned Mister E to face us. "Now, I didn't think much of it. Maybe you guys had something to do with Mr. Pocus's tomatoes, maybe you didn't. To tell you the truth, it's not high on my list of priorities. Anyway, I just received a phone call from the station. It seems that somebody has broken into the police storage shed and removed evidence."

"A real crime scene?" Shanks said eagerly. "Can we see it?"

Portnoy ignored the question, asking his own instead. "Do you know what the thieves took?" He patted the top of Mister E's head. "All of this little fella's friends. About three hundred little rubber duckies."

"We didn't steal any ducks!" Shanks cried out.

"Then where'd this guy come from?"

Shanks bit her lip. "Well, we stole *that one* duck. But not from the storage shed! From Mr. Babbage's backyard!"

"Mmm-hmm," Portnoy said skeptically. Then he turned serious. "I think we ought to have a little chat. Now, you kids are *not* under arrest. In fact, this isn't even an official police interview. If it was, I'd have to call your parents." He burped again and slid his gaze across the three of us. "And I'm guessing you guys aren't too eager to get them involved."

All three of us shook our heads simultaneously. Our parents getting a phone call from the police telling them we were suspects in multiple crimes was about as appealing as thumb-wrestling King Kong. Besides, we were innocent. We just needed to convince Portnoy of that.

"Okay, then. But I do have some questions for you. So let's call this a—*blarpuh!* Er, excuse me. Let's call this a friendly chat."

Portnoy placed Mister E back on the lean-to roof, then twirled around like a clumsy ballerina, surveying the surroundings for a good place to sit. When he didn't find any, he awkwardly folded himself into a cross-legged perch on the ground. The One and Onlys sank to our bottoms, too.

"Well, that was fun while it lasted," Peephole whimpered.

"The investigation?" I asked.

"No, my life," he said. "Looks like the rest of it will be spent in a jail cell."

My voice cracked as I pleaded, "I know it looks bad, Officer Portnoy, but we're completely innocent. In fact, we're investigating the duckies ourselves."

"You're . . . investigating?" Portnoy asked, shifting his weight around in an attempt to get more comfortable. He reached into his shirt pocket, felt around for a minute, and came out with a roll of Tums. He popped three into his mouth and crunched them loudly.

"That's right," Peephole said. "We're detectives."

"Is that so? Okay, kids, I want to believe you. So let's clear a few things up." He leaned forward, trying to rest his elbows on his knees. After a few seconds he thought better of it and leaned back again. "Let's start with Mr. Pocus's bushes. Do you know Mr. Pocus?"

Reluctantly we nodded. "He was our teacher," I said.

"Was he a good teacher?"

"Would Godzilla make a good house pet?" Peephole answered.

"*Peephole!*" Shanks hissed.

"What?" Peephole shot back defiantly. "Mr. Pocus was a horrible teacher. Everybody knows that. He made fourth grade fecl like a yearlong wet willie. Don't believe me? Go ask Antarctica Boy!"

"Who?" Portnoy grunted.

"Never mind," Peephole said. "Mr. Pocus is the worst. But we didn't touch his tomato plants."

"Then what were you doing in that neighborhood? And why are your knees and hands covered in dirt?"

The three of us exchanged looks. It seemed to me like we didn't have many options. "I think we should tell him everything," I said.

"That sounds like a good idea," Portnoy agreed.

"Okay, it goes like this," Shanks began, and she launched into the story of our investigation. She told him about the duckies and then went on to our visit with Babbage and the retrieval of Tina Fish, all the way through to the burial, which explained why we were dirty. When she left details out, Peephole and I supplied them. Portnoy crossed and recrossed his legs as he listened, tugging occasionally at his mustache. His eyebrows poked up a little when I mentioned what Babbage had to say about Mr. Pocus, specifically his Isaac Newton quote about getting what's coming to him.

When we were done, Portnoy squinted at us for a disconcertingly long time. I had to fight the urge to wave a hand in front of his face to make sure he hadn't fallen asleep with his eyes open. Finally, he said, "And if I call up Ms. Tuff, she'll confirm that you brought the fish to her this afternoon?"

We nodded.

"And if I called up your parents, they'd confirm that you were each at home last night?"

We nodded.

He sighed and stretched out his legs in front of him, speaking in a soft grumble: "I'll be straight with you kids. First of all, I don't much care about Pocus's tomatoes." His voice lowered to a whisper. "He's a grump. It's true. And between you and me, it's probably just an old-fashioned neighborly dispute. Second of all, I believe you. You haven't supplied me with any *real* evidence to absolve yourselves, so I'm not entirely sure why I believe you. But I do. Call it a hunch. Or maybe it's that your story is so weird that nobody could make it up."

The three of us breathed out deep sighs of relief.

He continued, "What interests me most is the duckies. Not how they got to Babbage's lawn to begin with, because that's not really a crime, is it?" His voice suddenly turned sharp. "But when somebody breaks into a police facility and steals our property"—he swung his fist down for emphasis, probably forgetting that he wasn't sitting at his desk—"now that's a crime worth investigating. And I don't think you kids had anything to do with it. For one, dispatch told me they found tire tracks leading away from the storage shed, and you aren't even close to being able to drive. She also told me the lock was destroyed. Seems like somebody took a hammer, or some other blunt object, and went to town on it until it broke. I hope you don't mind me saying this, but you don't strike me as hardened criminals." He was looking at Peephole, who had sweat pouring from his head like a leaky watering can.

"Thanks," I said, "for believing us."

"Somebody really wanted those duckies, huh?" Shanks said, jumping up to her feet. "But who? You got any leads? Want to compare notes? When do we get to see the crime scene?"

"You three? Never," Portnoy muttered, casting a stern look at Shanks.

"It sounds like a pretty complicated case," I said, trying a softer approach. "We're really good detectives. Maybe we could collaborate?"

A little smile poked out from under Portnoy's mustache. I'd seen that smile before: it meant he wasn't taking us seriously. "You kids let the real police do their work. I can assure you that—*blurf*—excuse me. I can assure you that we will handle—*blop.*" He raised a finger to his mouth and blew out a defeated sigh. "I'm working on a spicy bratwurst recipe for the Triple B this weekend," he explained with an embarrassed shrug. "I've always wanted to enter a dish, but I never thought I could do it. This year I figured, why not? But it's repeating on me. I think I—*bloomp*—know where I went wrong." He raised his index finger to emphasize his point. "See, there's too much hot sauce in the—" He stopped suddenly, aware that he might be giving us more information than we wanted.

"I understand," I said, feeling bad for the guy. "It's anybody's Bonanza."

"So what's the next step?" Peephole asked.

Portnoy raised his eyebrows and gave Peephole a curious look. "Well, for me, the next step is to head back to Mr. Pocus and report that I've investigated his damaged-property complaint and the results are inconclusive. Since he's the chief taster at the Triple B and I don't want to make him mad, I have to find a way to politely tell him that we probably won't ever find out who tore up his tomato plants and that I won't be spending any more of my time investigating it."

"Good plan," Peephole said, sounding as if he was one of Officer Portnoy's deputies. "And what about us?"

"As for you," Portnoy said, clambering from a squat to a stand, "there is one thing I think you should do. Go home and take a shower. All of you." He pinched his nose. "Somebody here smells like a dead fish."

A Race Downtown

Portnoy had barely disappeared from view when Shanks catapulted up. "Come on! We don't have much time!"

Peephole blinked at her. "Where are you going?"

"Where do you think? To the police station!" She was hopping in place, but Peephole and I didn't budge. "Didn't you hear Portnoy? He's heading back to talk to Pocus. If we're going to investigate the break-in at the storage shed, we have to go now, before he gets back!"

"Didn't *you* hear Portnoy?" Peephole countered. "He said to stay away from the storage shed. We could get in real trouble if he catches us meddling with a crime scene."

"But how do you expect us to solve the case if we don't evaluate the clues ourselves? We have to take some risks, Peephole!" Shanks said, her voice practically a whine as she edged toward her bike. "Paul, what do you think?"

There it was: I was usually the tiebreaker in their arguments, and now it was up to me. I bit my lip and considered the situation. Peephole was right, of course: it would be bad news for the One and Onlys if Portnoy caught us noodling with the crime scene. Our solving the case of the duckies would be pretty much impossible if we were all grounded for life. On the other hand, I agreed with Shanks. What kind of detectives would we be if we didn't try to at least get a look at the storage shed? After all, if we were serious about solving this mystery—and I knew I was—this was the only way we could make it happen.

"If we're going to get there before Portnoy," I said, rising to my feet and running toward my bike, "we'll need to take some shortcuts. Follow me!"

As we pushed our bikes through the tall grass out to the road, I noticed that the little wooden stakes with pink ribbons were lining the perimeter of the whole field now. And I saw something else. It was a small sign, poking up from the grass. In neat black letters, it read THE CONQUISTADOR IS COMING.

Seeing the sign sent a little tremble through my body. Hadn't my parents been whispering about "conquistador"? But now wasn't the time to contemplate this new development. We were in a race with Portnoy to get to the police station. I made a mental note to investigate the Conquistador more thoroughly when I had more time.

By now, Portnoy was probably walking up to Pocus's

front door. Luckily, nobody knew the secret pathways of Bellwood better than me. First, I busted a quick right into the Sanchez's driveway, my bike squeaking crazily down the pavement. In second grade, I went to Buddy Sanchez's house for a birthday party. The clown who was hired to entertain us accidentally crashed his car into the basketball hoop in Buddy's driveway. We all thought it was part of the act. When the clown got out of the car, twirled for a minute, and then collapsed on the front lawn, we all clapped. I guess it was pretty hard to drive in size twenty-five shoes.

Buddy's backyard connected to a hidden path that spat you out onto the Winklers' driveway, which led to Rory Drive. We zipped by Dr. Dave's Ice Cream Parlor, which had the second-best rocky road in town. Dave, who was not a doctor, turned from wiping down the window and gave us a quick salute. From there, we pedaled through the elementary school playground, then past the water tower that always reminded me of a Martian tripod waiting to attack. Next, we cut through the parking lot of my family's very own Honest Hardware, just as Bella Tuff was getting into her old blue pickup truck, which barked like a sick sea lion when she started it. And as they always had ever since I'd known her, her brakes squealed so bad that I could still hear them even from a block away.

Finally, we reached the Bellwood police and fire station. We whipped around to the side and skidded up to the ramshackle little building located behind the station.

It had flaking navy-blue paint and a sun-bleached roof. My legs burned and my lungs were aching, but we'd made it in record time. And here we were, about to investigate our first real crime scene. All three of us swiveled our heads to and fro to make sure Portnoy was nowhere in sight. We let our bikes rattle to the ground and trotted over to the shed.

"Tire tracks!" Shanks shouted, and then immediately put a hand over her mouth, remembering that we were trying *not* to draw attention to ourselves.

"They lead right up to the shed," she continued in a high whisper.

A set of tire tracks zigzagged across the dusty dirt road that led from the storage shed, around the station, and to the road.

"Looks like somebody couldn't make up their mind," she said, squatting down and inspecting the tracks up close.

"What do you mean by that?" I asked.

"These tracks." She pointed. "They're all over the place. It's not just a straight line. See?" She stood and walked a wayward pattern, tracing the edges of the tire tracks in the dirt. "My guess is the driver pulled up to the shed, then decided they would rather have the back of their vehicle against the door."

"I think you're right," I said. "That would make it easier to load all of the duckies, if the person was driving a pickup truck."

"And it would allow for a faster getaway," Peephole added. "They could just hop in their truck and go."

"And that's not all." Shanks was on a roll. "Look at all these short track marks. Only a couple of feet here in this direction, then a few feet in that direction. Seems like they did a lot of reversing for a pretty simple turn-around. And look!" She hurried over to a cement post at the edge of a dirt path, and bent down to inspect something on the ground. "Broken red glass!"

"Broken red glass?" Peephole repeated slowly, pulling absentmindedly at his ear. "I've got it! What if it's from some expensive piece of jewelry that the thief was wearing? And what if it broke while they were stealing the ducks? Or what if the thief wears red-tinted glasses, and they fell and smashed during the robbery? All we need to do is find a person who is . . . uh . . . *not* wearing red glasses. Or wait . . . um. . . ."

Shanks scratched her nose. "Actually, I think it's from a taillight. The thief probably bumped his truck against this cement pole." She leaned in close to the pole. "Look! There are scratches of green paint here. That must be where the truck's bumper backed into it."

"Oh . . . yeah," Peephole agreed, but he was clearly deflated.

"It was a good idea, though," I offered, but Peephole didn't look like he wanted my encouragement.

"Let's take a look at the busted lock," I suggested.

We huddled around the door to the shed, which had a latch rather than a doorknob. The paint around the latch was chipped more than the rest of the door, and a broken padlock was on the ground.

"Somebody really did a number on this lock," I said.

Shanks whistled. "A lock like this would require a lot of force to break, and with something heavy. A hammer is my guess."

Suddenly, the door to the shed swung open from the inside, and the three of us fell back onto the ground, startled. A pair of muddy sneakers stood before us. I followed the legs up to see a familiar figure standing in the doorway, a stack of little orange training cones in her hands, and her short black hair poking out from the bottom of a yellow baseball cap.

"Janice?" I said.

"Paul? Is that you?" My neighbor and old babysitter peered down at the three of us with her forest-green eyes and a curious grin. Her red T-shirt and yellow cap had the same words printed on them in block letters: BELLWOOD FIRE DEPARTMENT. "What are you guys doing here?"

"Uh . . ." I wracked my brain to come up with a good excuse for snooping around the police storage shed. I shot desperate glances at Peephole and Shanks, but they just returned them. "Are those . . . cones?" was all I could manage.

"Yep," Janice said, taking the dumb question in stride.

"We're helping Byron set up for our field exercises." She stepped aside, and through the door we could see several other kids wearing the same red shirt and yellow cap, unloading more cones from a row of lockers against the opposite wall. "Oh! You guys must be here to sign up for the Bellwood Junior Firefighters. Is that it? It's really fun!"

Behind me, the sound of a car door slamming caught my attention. I turned to see Officer Portnoy standing next to his police cruiser, arching his back and stretching his arms to the sky. He removed his hat and scratched the top of his head. With a fist to his chest, he burped.

"Junior Firefighters?" Peephole repeated inquisitively. "Actually, we're here to—"

"That's right!" I cut him off. "We're here to sign up!" I hopped to my feet, pulling Peephole and Shanks up as well. "Well, we're here to learn more about the Junior Firefighters. And then we'll decide if we want to join." I shuffled us all past Janice into the shed, out of Portnoy's line of vision.

"What are you doing?" Peephole whispered, annoyed at being yanked around like a dog on a leash.

"Portnoy's back," I said quietly enough so Janice couldn't hear. "This will be our cover story if he sees us."

Janice stepped back into the shed with us. She was smiling. "Well, I understand why you're interested in joining. The forest fires this summer have kinda freaked me out, too. When the air starts to get smoky, I feel so helpless, like there's nothing I can do. But then I realized I *can* do something, and that's why I'm here."

"That's cool," Shanks said, with genuine admiration in her voice. "So you guys are, like, out there fighting the fires?"

"Yeah!" Janice said, then cocked her head. "Well, not me, or any of the other recruits. We're mostly doing drills and exercises." She pointed the cones in her hand at a tall red-headed teenager. "Byron is the son of the fire chief, and he's the chief of the Junior Firefighters. He's done some training in the helicopters with the real firefighters!"

"Awesome," Peephole said, staring at Byron.

"Yeah, hopefully someday I'll get a chance to do something like that, too." Janice looked at me and smiled. "So, Paul, are your parents getting ready for the Triple B?"

I chuckled. "It seems like they've been getting ready their whole lives. But, yeah, they're taking it pretty seriously this year."

She rolled her eyes sympathetically. "My parents are, too. For some reason, they think this is going to be their year. Hey, Byron!" she called out, and the nest of red hair turned to us. "Here are a few potential recruits who want to talk to you!" She turned back to us. "I gotta get going, but it was good to see you again, Paul."

I waved goodbye.

Byron motioned for us to come closer. We crossed the storage shed, passing several Junior Firefighters who were following Janice with cones in their arms. Byron stood in front of an open locker that held a random assortment of things: a whistle, a deflated rubber ball, a pair of mud-caked shoes, a Frisbee. Taped to the inside of the door was a photograph of a little boy wearing a plastic firefighter's helmet, sitting on a woman's lap. I recognized the woman as Mrs. Willis, the chief of the fire department, which meant that the little boy was Byron himself.

"I guess you've always wanted to be a firefighter," I said, pointing to the picture.

Byron closed the locker and grinned down at us, his face crinkling with concentration, as if he was trying to remember where he knew us from.

"Byron Willis," he said, extending a huge hand to shake. "So you want to join the Junior Firefighters?"

"Shanks," Shanks announced herself and allowed her little hand to be engulfed by Byron's. "This is Peephole, and this is Paul."

Byron looked at me. "Just Paul?"

I sighed. "Paul's enough."

"I thought this was supposed to be the police storage shed, not the fire department's," Shanks said, trying to sound as casual as possible.

"It's both, actually," Byron said, looking around as if noticing where he was for the first time. "We share pretty much everything—this shed, some of the vehicles. We even share the station, though there's a hallway separating us."

The One and Onlys nodded and surveyed the space. It was a dusty room, one side of which was half filled with un-marked boxes, ladders, and coiled hoses. I guessed that was the fire department's stash of equipment. On the other side was a pile of random stuff: smashed mailboxes, bent road signs, a porta-potty that looked like it had been dragged behind a car for a mile or two.

"Police evidence," Byron explained, following our eyes. "Mostly broken or vandalized property—things that people don't really want to get back. Hey, I know you guys from somewhere, don't I?"

Peephole extended a hand. "We saw you yesterday at Babbage's house. You know, the ducks."

"Oh, yeah." Byron shook Peephole's hand. "So is Peephole your real name?"

"No, it's Alexander. See, I had this teacher—Mr. Pocus— and he used to call me Beanpole and—"

"I had Mr. Pocus, too," Byron said in a sympathetic voice. "He called me Carrot-Top."

"He did? Because you liked to eat carrots?"

"*Peephole!*" Shanks said. "Because of his red hair!"

"Oh, yeah," Peephole said. "Anyway, being in that guy's class was like torture, except worse. You can always cry 'uncle' if you want the torture to stop. But fourth grade lasted forever."

"You're telling me."

Peephole sighed. "Did you hear the rumor about Antarctica Boy?"

Byron drew his lower lip under his front teeth. Finally, he said, "Yeah, but it's not true. I didn't move to Antarctica."

"You?" I interjected.

Byron turned to look at me. "Fourth grade was tough for me. I hated getting up every morning and going to school. I didn't move to Antarctica, but I did stay home for two weeks, and started seeing a counselor."

"Pocus is such a jerk," Peephole said, and then a sly grin bloomed on his face. "Want to hear something funny?" He leaned in closer to Byron. "Somebody tore up his prized tomato plants. We're pretty sure it was Mr. Babbage."

Byron's eyebrows rose in surprise, and then he slipped into a smirk. "Well, I'm not one for revenge," he said, "but that *is* pretty funny. Seeing his sneering mug yesterday brought back some memories, and not good ones. I almost mistook him for one of those mean little garden gnomes he has in his backyard."

Peephole ruptured into a giggle, but his joy was interrupted by a booming noise outside. *WOCK WOCK WOCK.* The walls of the shed started to tremble with the sound of a helicopter directly overhead. We ran outside in time to see a long red-and-yellow helicopter touching down in the field behind the station. The pilot cut the engine, and the blades slowed to a stop.

"That's one of the choppers we're using to fight the fires outside of town," explained Byron, who'd followed us outside. "We fly over the flames and dump water on them. It's pretty cool." He spoke with obvious pride.

"So you've been out to the fire?" I asked.

"Well," he hesitated, "not yet. I'm still training in the

chopper, but I have dumped some practice loads out in the open land below town."

"Moo-Landia," Peephole said.

"Huh?"

"Never mind," I said quickly, suddenly embarrassed by our childish nickname for the land below Highway 43. "That's still pretty awesome, even if you haven't actually been to the fire."

From behind us came a series of angry grunts that reminded me of the noises Ronald made when he dreamed about chasing squirrels. We whirled around in time to see Portnoy huffing and puffing toward us with a full head of steam.

"You!" he barked, a finger extended in our direction.

"Officer Portnoy," I started, hands up, "we can explain."

But as he stomped closer, it was clear his finger was pointing at Byron. "What do you think you're doing, letting civilians trample my crime scene?"

Byron took a step back, clearly caught off guard by Portnoy's anger. "Crime scene? I—I—I don't know what you're talking about."

Portnoy made a point of looking around the shed before saying, "Somebody broke in here last night and removed evidence! And I haven't even had a chance to investigate yet!"

"I swear I had no idea," Byron said, and I felt bad for him. His face was a shade or two darker than his hair, and his eyes were wide with fear.

"And you kids," Portnoy said, finally turning his fury to us. "I thought I told you to leave the detective work to the professionals."

"We are!" I said. "We were here talking with Byron about joining the Junior Firefighters! We promise!"

Portnoy shot Byron a fierce look.

"It's true," he said. "I was telling them about how we're fighting the forest fires."

"We're not trying to get involved in the investigation," Shanks said, shaking her head. "But since you brought it up, I'll tell you one thing: it looks like you're dealing with a pretty awful driver."

"Now you listen here," Portnoy began, but then he fell silent and his brow furrowed. "What do you mean by that?"

"Look," Shanks said, showing him the zigzag of the tire tracks, the paint on the pole, the glass from the broken taillight.

"Huh," Portnoy grunted. He stroked his mustache, rolling his eyes from Shanks to the ground and back to Shanks again. "You might be right about that awful driver, Chunk."

"Shanks," she corrected.

"You're welcome," Portnoy said.

"And there's the smashed lock." I pointed to the twisted metal lock on the ground. "Somebody really let this thing have it."

"Somebody broke into the shed?" Byron sounded astonished. "What would anyone want with all those duckies?"

"That's what we're going to figure out!" I said. Portnoy shot me a look. "I mean, that's what *he's* going to figure out."

"And look!" Peephole added excitedly. "There's another set of tracks."

He was right. We all bent down and peered at the dirt.

"These are smaller, from a different vehicle," Shanks said. "Could there be an accomplice?"

Portnoy shook his head. "Those tracks match the tires on the department's van. They must be from when I drove up yesterday morning to unload the ducks. See how the other tracks go over them? That means whoever it was was here after me."

"Good detective work, chief!" Shanks said.

It was her turn to get a sideways look from Portnoy.

"Well, I've got some training exercises to lead," Byron said. "Good luck with the investigation, Officer Portnoy." He turned to us. "Are you guys coming? We're about to do some long-distance running to improve our lung capacity."

"As a matter of fact," Peephole replied, visibly uncomfortable at the mention of exercise. "I've got to get home. My mom's pregnant, so there's probably some chore that she wants me to do."

"Me too," Shanks said. "Not about the pregnant mom, but about the chores. There are always chores."

Byron looked down at me.

"Chores," I echoed lamely. "But thanks for talking to us. We'll seriously consider joining the team."

Byron flashed a thumbs-up, then turned and loped off toward the field, his big hands and feet seeming too heavy for his wiry frame. When he got close to the crowd of Junior Firefighters, he barked orders that we couldn't hear, and they fell in line behind him. We watched as they jogged around the field in a weaving pattern, in and out of cones, like a long red-and-yellow snake.

"I'll admit it, kids," Portnoy said, and we all turned to look at him. "This ducky business is all a bit"—he spread his hands out—"mysterious. But there's a perfectly logical explanation for the whole thing. You see, Bellwood is a normal little town, and things like this"—he pointed to the shed—"don't usually happen here. Don't worry. I'll get to the bottom of it."

"If you need our help, you know where to find us," Shanks said. "We'd be honored to join the Bellwood Police Junior Detective Force."

"Well, that doesn't exist," Portnoy grumbled. "And anyway, I think I'll be okay." He tapped his forehead with a stubby finger and winked. "You see, Chunk, I've got a mind like a steel trap. Nothing gets in."

"Um . . . don't you mean 'out'?" I asked.

"That's what I said, Macaroni. Nothing gets out."

Moonlight Serenade

I couldn't sleep. The past two days had been astronomically odd, and my mind was racing with too many questions for me to be able to relax. I knew Portnoy was wrong about one thing: Bellwood was *not* a normal town. Normal towns didn't have lawns that sprouted rubber duckies out of thin air. In normal towns, being the bratwurst champion did not make you a target. Even if the One and Onlys were the only people that recognized it, Bellwood was a far cry from normal.

I threw my covers off, tiptoed to my window so as not to wake my parents, and gently raised it. With a crouch and a squirm, I was sitting on the roof, looking out over Munchaus Avenue. My block, and probably all of Bellwood, was dark and deathly quiet. A single window in a house three doors down flickered with blue TV light, and the faint smell of smoke from the forest fires wafted in the breeze. A ragged red-orange moon hung in the sky, glowing dimly through the haze. It was probably because of the smoke, but it felt like the whole night was an old photograph that somebody had smudged.

There was something in the air that made me feel restless. Just like I had the night before, I thought of the duckies in Babbage's yard, but now there was a new wrinkle in their mystery. They had disappeared from the police storage shed as strangely as they had arrived in Babbage's yard. I remembered the smashed lock on the ground outside the shed. Somebody in Bellwood was responsible for those duckies showing up and for them disappearing. But who? And what did it all mean? Again I was smacked with the feeling that things were happening in Bellwood that I didn't understand. Were they good or bad? Maybe Portnoy said it best. They were . . . *mysterious.*

And then, just like the night before, there was movement across the street. The door on the side of the Wagners' garage slowly creaked open, and Janice appeared, wheeling her electric scooter into the driveway. On her back was an enormous mass, and at first, through the film of the smoky night, it looked like she'd sprouted a grotesque hunchback. With a swift push, she propelled her scooter down the driveway and then curved left, toward the overgrown forest road that led into the Bell Woods.

I willed myself invisible, knowing that it would take only

a quick glance up in my direction for her to see me. Something about the way she kept flicking her head back toward her house gave me the distinct impression that what she was doing was supposed to be a secret. Her scooter let out a low mechanical whirr as she passed by my house, and I squinted and saw that it wasn't a hunchback at all but a big black carrying case. *It's her tuba,* I thought, remembering that she'd had it on her back when I saw her at Babbage's.

But where would she be going with her tuba at this hour? Into the Bell Woods, apparently. The scooter let out a little rattle and groan as she drove it from the pavement of Munchaus Avenue up onto the overgrown grass of the old forest road. A tiny *flick* rang out in the night, and the scooter's headlight popped on, casting a thin shaft of pale light into the darkness of the forest. And then, with its whirr and rattling becoming fainter to my ear, the scooter carried Janice and her tuba into the woods.

My uncertainty lasted only a moment. During that second or two, I had the fleeting wish that Shanks and Peephole were there so that we could all follow Janice into the unknown darkness. But before I realized what I was doing, I grabbed my phone and found myself tiptoeing across my bedroom, down the stairs, and past a snoring Ronald. I stuffed my feet into my sneakers and threw a hoodie over my shoulder before slipping out the front door into the night. Pausing at the edge of my lawn, I considered going back to get my bike. It would be faster, of course, but its squeak would be too loud. It would give me away in a second. I put my head down and ran faster and headed into the tall grass of the forest service road. Janice had a head start, and she was on an electric scooter, but that also meant that she'd be easier to track. Sure enough, up ahead in the cleared-out alley between the trees, I could see her headlight bumping up and down on the uneven road.

I huffed and puffed to keep up with her. After a minute or two my lungs ached from breathing in the thick, smoky air. I fought back a cough, knowing that any noise might give me away. All around me the black outline of the woods seemed to grow taller and taller, and I could have sworn that I heard sighing coming from the tree line. Once again, I silently wished that Peephole and Shanks were there with me. Shanks wouldn't have been afraid at all, which would have made me feel better, and Peephole would have been way more scared than me, which also would have made me feel better. But my curiosity was stronger than my fear, and I pressed on after Janice. Where was she leading me? How deep into the Bell Woods were we going to plunge? Luckily, I didn't have to wonder much longer. The scooter's headlight veered off from the forest road to the left and came to an abrupt stop.

I slowed to a trot and tried to make my footfalls as soft as possible as I approached. Soon I was close enough to see that Janice had stopped in a clearing off the forest road. She'd flipped the kickstand down and was standing a few feet in front of the scooter, her big tuba case illuminated by the single headlight. Keeping my eyes fixed on the case, I crept forward, carefully measuring every stride. A curious sinking feeling accompanied each step, and I realized with surprise that the hard dirt and grass of the forest road had given way to a spongy forest floor. My sneakers were sinking into the ground, every footfall taking me deeper into a muddy patch.

Great, I thought. *We're in the middle of a drought, but Janice has led me to the only swamp in Bellwood.*

If I could get a little closer, I figured I might be able to tell what she was up to. I tried to control my heavy breathing, but the run had taken a toll on me. A single bead of sweat rolled from my forehead onto the tip of my nose, and I reached up to wipe it away. Now I was close enough to see tiny particles of ash floating in the beam of the scooter's headlight.

I took another step and my foot sank into the mud, suddenly throwing me off balance. My hand jutted out for support and found a thin branch poking out from the trunk of a nearby tree.

Snap. The sound of the branch breaking in my hand echoed through the silent woods. I froze and held my breath. What would happen if Janice saw me? What kind of excuse could I possibly have for being in the woods? I swallowed that fear, remembering that Janice was the one who had led me here. If anybody needed to explain herself, it was Janice.

But if she heard the snap, she didn't react. In fact, she'd

remained as still as a statue since the moment I had her in view. I watched her and counted to five, but she didn't move so much as a finger in that time. It was as if she'd seen something that had turned her into stone. Leaning to the right, I craned my neck to get a glimpse of what she might have been looking at, but a low snarl of tree limbs blocked my view. With intense concentration, I noiselessly shuffled a few feet to my left to get a better look.

And there they were . . . looking every bit as strange and out of place in the electric blue of the scooter light as they had in Babbage's yard, their round little heads and swooping tails bubbling up like some alien growth from the mud of the swamp. I couldn't believe my eyes. I'd found the duckies. But what on earth were they doing here? In a random patch of mud in the Bell Woods?

Or, rather, Janice had found the duckies. And judging by the way she still hadn't budged, I wondered whether she had been expecting the odd little visitors to be here or was as surprised to find them as I was. The two of us stayed very still for what seemed like a long time, staring warily at the unexplainable pile of duckies, as if they might pop to life and start waddling toward us under the smoke-soaked red moon.

Finally, Janice turned, reached up, and lowered her tuba case to the ground. With careful and precise motions, as if she were a heart surgeon going in for the first incision, she kneeled down and unzipped the case, the sound of the zipper amplified by the silence of the woods. With equal care, she grasped her tuba, whose golden brassiness glinted in the scooter's headlight, and lifted it to playing position.

A long moment passed. Janice stood with the mouthpiece of her tuba hovering near her lips as she stared at the ducks, and I crouched behind her, close enough to toss a paper airplane by her ear.

She stared at the ducks. I stared at her staring at the ducks. And then I, too, was staring at the ducks.

And then things seemed to happen in slow motion. Janice expelled three heavy breaths, then bobbed her head four times with exaggerated intensity, like a rock drummer counting off a beat, before sliding backward on one foot while kicking up her opposite leg in the air. At the same instant, a low booming rumble poured out of her tuba, reverberating off the enormous trees all around us and startling me into a crouch. From there, behind the trunk of a thick tree, I watched the strangest performance I'd ever seen.

Janice moved like a robot ballerina, her legs twisting and planting, twisting and planting. Each of her steps sent up a sloshing *gulp* from the swampy mud, and occasionally her whole body would twirl, tuba and all, like an Olympic figure skater. Sometimes, one knee would shoot up in one direction while the other fanned out away from it. Somehow she kept her balance. But it was more than just that. She was making a mockery of the laws of physics, all while blowing out a clear and resounding tune from her enormous tuba. In fact, I recognized the song: "We Are the Champions."

Entranced by the moonlight serenade, I forgot to blink or even breathe. I had a fleeting idea of pulling out my phone and recording everything, but I didn't want to risk the movement, and anyway it would be too dark for the camera to pick anything up without the flash on. At the end of the song, Janice leapt into a scissors kick, then dropped to one knee, allowing the final note to ring out. When my trance broke in the still-echoing quiet that followed, I had to resist the urge to clap. I'd blow my cover, of course, but the ducks weren't going to give her applause, and neither was the blood-red moon looking down on us.

I stayed very still as Janice stood, caught her breath for a minute or two, then launched back into the same routine, from the beginning. It was as flawless and mesmerizing as the first time. And so was the next time she did it. And the next time. And the time after that. For what must have been fifteen minutes, I watched as she practiced her movements again and again.

Finally, out of breath and apparently satisfied, she bent down, zipped her tuba into its case, and threw it over her shoulders as she stood up. She walked her scooter back toward the forest road. Before kicking off, she slowly turned and regarded the pile of duckies one last time. Now that the glow of the scooter's headlight was no longer upon them, they were easy to miss. But I knew they were there, just radiating mystery, and so did Janice.

Without warning, Janice whipped around and looked in my direction. I ducked my head as fast as I could. Had she seen me? Was she going to call out my name, demand to know why I was spying on her? To my relief, a few seconds later the whirring sound of her scooter filled the woods again, and I saw her move back down the forest road toward Munchaus Avenue, and toward another "ordinary" summer night in Bellwood.

By the time I made it to the forest road, the scooter's headlight was a thin point of light way in the distance. I didn't care. I knew where she was going, and it was the same place I was headed. Back to bed.

Somehow I wasn't scared on my walk out of the Bell Woods to my house, even though the black silhouettes of the trees seemed to lean in toward me, reaching out spindly fingers into the smeary sky. I guess I was just too excited. There was a real mystery to solve in Bellwood, and it kept getting weirder and weirder—and better and better.

When I could no longer see the scooter light ahead of me, I pulled my phone out. I texted Shanks and Peephole.

U guys up? Cuz I've got a story you're not gonna believe!

⇒ 10 ⇐

Not a Who but a What

"Bratwurst, bratwurst. How come you're so yummy?" My dad two-stepped his way into the living room, singing off-key. "Bratwurst, bratwurst. Bonanza in my tummy!" He had been singing variations of this song every day for the last week.

I looked up from my notebook and blinked at him. I was a little groggy from missing so much sleep the night before, but I was also electrified by the new developments in the case of the duckies. I pictured Janice, swaying and kicking and sliding through a mud patch in the middle of the Bell Woods, serenading the duckies—and me—under a blood-red moon. Part of me wondered if I'd dreamed up the whole thing.

I'd been scribbling down my scattered thoughts on the recent events in Bellwood. If I could make sense of all the clues and suspects, then maybe the One and Onlys could crack the case. When we talked to Babbage, he seemed certain that his neighbor, Mr. Pocus, was responsible for the ducks. The two of them definitely had bad blood, but was that enough to explain everything? There was also Bella Tuff, who told us that the fish in Babbage's yard had come from Schuylerville Lake. But Peephole didn't trust her. And, it's true, she *did* have a ducky on her desk. But she didn't have a motive, as far as I could tell. Why would she dump duckies in Babbage's yard, and then break into the police storage shed, remove them, and dump them once again in a swamp in the Bell Woods?

In my notebook I wrote THE BREAK-IN and underlined it. Whoever took the duckies from the storage shed was not afraid to break the law—not to mention a padlock. I tapped my pencil against the page, feeling a tiny tug that we had missed something when we were there. But what? There were the big clues of the tire tracks, the broken taillight, and the green paint on the cement pole outside the shed door. Was there something else right under our noses?

But who, then? Janice? She had led me to the duckies, after all, and she was also there in the storage shed yesterday when we investigated it. But I couldn't believe that she was involved. I didn't *want* to believe it. And yet, how could she explain last night's mysterious performance?

I had to fight the urge to tell my parents about the investigation. This was already the most exciting summer

I'd ever had, and it felt weird to keep all of it from my mom and dad. But telling them the details of the case would mean admitting that I'd been sneaking around town in the middle of the night. They would get worried, and mad, and they might even ground me. Knowing them, they could do something crazy like call Peephole's and Shanks's parents, and then all the One and Onlys would get grounded. I couldn't risk shutting down the investigation, especially now that the mystery was getting deeper.

"What are you working on there, Paul?" My dad peered down at me with a particular look that I was very familiar with. He was thinking of a job for me to do.

"I'm, uh, working on a case," I said, which was the truth.

"A case?"

"I'm going to solve the mystery of the ducks. You know, in Mr. Babbage's yard."

"Ah, yes. Let me *quack* the case for you, Paul," he said with a wink, just to make sure I got his pun. "It was just a prank. And speaking of yards . . . I couldn't help but notice that our *own* yard is only partly mowed."

"Oh . . . yeah. I guess I got distracted. I'll finish it today."

My mom, doing yoga in the den, overheard us and called out her agreement with dad's conclusion. "Crazy teenagers!" she shouted from her downward-dog position.

My parents thought everything was a prank pulled by crazy teenagers. That spring, for instance, when a thunderstorm knocked out the power for the whole neighborhood, they combed the area with flashlights trying to find the goons responsible for it.

I wanted to tell my parents about our progress in the case, but another part of me wanted to keep it secret. I guess I wanted the One and Onlys to solve the case all on our own. Also, they'd have a nuclear meltdown if they knew we had been questioned by Officer Portnoy, even if we were completely innocent. Besides, Bella Tuff was on our suspect list, and that would be hard to explain to my dad.

And that reminded me: "Shouldn't you be at work, Dad? It's almost nine."

"I'm taking the morning off," he explained. "Your mother and I have to work on our recipe for the Triple B. Bella's doing me a favor and watching the store."

With a cringe, I remembered how rude Peephole had been to Bella the day before. But what *was* she hiding? "So, um . . . Bella said she missed work on Tuesday."

My dad nodded. "That's right. Her first sick day in ten years. By the way, after you kids left yesterday, she grumbled something about needing to get a lock for her office door. What were you talking to her about, anyway?"

"Oh, we . . . uh . . ." I wracked my brain to come up with a good lie, but nothing came. "We had a couple of questions about a fish and, um, the ducks."

"Prank!" my mom called from the den, still stuck on the duckies.

I walked to the doorway, grateful for an excuse to dodge my dad's questions about Bella, and found my mom contorting her body into a pretzel. "It's because kids don't know what to do with themselves these days," she said. "Too much time on their hands!"

"And what did you guys do when you were that age?" I asked skeptically.

My mom thought about this. "Not much," she admitted. "Drove around. Ate French fries. Saw movies at the old drive-in theater. Your father and I used to go there all the time. We had our first date there. Remember, Jerry?"

"Oh, I remember, Denise." My dad squeezed by me into the den. He had a faint grin on his face, like he was reliving the best years of his life in his head. "It used to be *the* thing to do on weekends."

"It was the *only* thing to do," my mom said, balancing on her head.

"How long has the drive-in movie theater been abandoned, anyway?" I asked.

"*Looong* time," my mom said.

"You know"—my dad snapped his fingers—"we used to have a picture of your mom and me at the drive-in when we were young." He disappeared from the room, and I listened as he opened and closed drawers.

"Aha!" he called out, and returned holding a dusty high school yearbook.

"This is from our freshman year," he said with a wonky

grin on his face. He flipped through the pages for a few seconds, then handed the book to me as he beamed with pride. There they were, my mom and dad, standing in front of a red convertible that probably wasn't even theirs. In the background of the photograph were rows of cars and people milling about. My dad was right, they were much younger in the picture; he had a mesh blue baseball hat on, from which fluffy tufts of brown hair poked out, and my mom's hair was curly and tall. They both wore great big toothy smiles. It was funny that they'd gotten older but still had the exact same way of smiling. Maybe that never changes, from the time you're a baby all the way to the retirement home.

"So why did the drive-in close down?" I asked as I absent-mindedly flipped through the pages of the old yearbook.

My dad shrugged. "Times changed. A big multiplex opened up in Swenson City, and everybody started going there instead. After a while, Mr. Shamtraw must not have wanted to put the money in to keep it open."

"But I thought everybody loved the drive-in. Why would they go to Swenson City instead?"

My mom and dad exchanged a glance. "The drive-in was old, even when we were going to it," she explained. "It had been around forever. Your grandparents used to go there. And the new theater was bigger. It had comfortable seats. It was shiny."

"Shiny?"

"It was new, and it was convenient," she said.

"But what about all the good times people had at the drive-in? Didn't that mean anything?"

My dad put a hand on my shoulder. "Of course it meant something. That field will always have a magic feeling about it. But if it's a question of nostalgia or convenience, people choose convenience. Every time."

"That's stupid," I said. Again I couldn't help but feel bad for the drive-in.

My dad's sad smile said two things. (1) He agreed with me. He *really* did. And (2) there wasn't anything we could do about it.

Just then I caught my parents giving each other another heavy look. Their eyes met and held for a nanosecond too long to be normal, and I thought I detected a hint of worry in their faces.

Somehow I knew they wouldn't tell me what was wrong. I decided to ask a different question, one that I suspected was more to the point.

"Who is the Conquistador?"

Alarm flashed on their faces.

"Where'd you hear about the Conquistador?" my dad asked.

"I saw a sign at the drive-in field that said he was coming soon."

"It's not a who—it's a what," my mom explained. "The Conquistador is a megastore."

"A what?"

"You know, like a Walmart. A giant store that has every-thing. Groceries, clothes, sporting goods."

"Hardware," my dad added.

"And they're building it right here in Bellwood?" I asked. "Where the drive-in used to be?" *And where the headquarters of the One and Onlys currently is located,* I thought. I remem-bered the two people in hard hats pounding stakes into the ground.

"That's right," my dad said. "Construction is set to begin this week."

"Why does the Conquistador have to be built *right* there?" I said, aware that my voice had a whiny pitch to it. "I mean, couldn't they build it somewhere else and keep the field the way it is?"

"That space isn't being used right now. And, well, it *is* a good location. It's going to be very hard for our little store to compete with it," my dad continued, and there was something strange about his voice. He sounded so . . . defeated.

"But people will still go to Honest Hardware. They've been shopping at our store for generations. Right?"

My mom forced a smile. "Sure they will. Some of them, at least. The loyal ones."

"But everybody in Bellwood shops there. They'll all be loyal, won't they?"

My dad sighed. "You know, yesterday Darrel Sullivan came into the store."

"The dude with the white goatee? Yeah, I think I re-member seeing him." I looked back down at the yearbook. I'd flipped to the prom page. The prom king and queen, an awkwardly hugging couple in a matching baby-blue suit and dress, beamed their billboard-sized smiles up at me.

"Yep," my dad said. "Darrel's a decent guy, but he can't seem to hang on to a job for very long. He's got a million get-rich-quick schemes, but none of them pan out. In the last couple of years, he's tried everything from putting on magic shows to breeding rabbits to making furniture. He even tried his hand at giving tennis lessons."

"I didn't know Darrel was an athlete," my mom said.

"He's not," my dad replied. "Which is why he's now a truck driver for a toy company. It's the steadiest job he's had in a long time. Anyway, he lives right around the cor-ner from the store, on Radford, so he comes in fairly often to pick up whatever random thing he might need for his current job, and yesterday he looked particularly frazzled. His eyes were all bloodshot, like he hadn't slept all night, and he was sweating buckets. I really wanted to help him out, but I didn't have what he needed." He shoved his hands into his pockets helplessly.

While listening to my dad, I ran my fingers along the glossy pages of the yearbook. On the opposite page from the prom king and queen was a photo collage of other stu-dents at the dance: a goofy dude with wavy hair squeezing his date, which was a stuffed dog; a group of girls, their arms around each other, laughing as if they'd just heard the funniest joke ever told; a guy in an immaculate tuxedo with perfectly combed black hair, smiling down at his date, a curly haired girl wearing a T-shirt that read GONE FISHING. My eyes lingered on this last couple. There was something so familiar about them. Was it the self-assured gleam in the guy's eye? Was it the way the girl's hair seemed to explode from her head? And then it hit me.

I yelped. "Bella Tuff and Mr. Babbage went to prom together!"

My mom leaned over and squinted at the yearbook. "Would you look at that! I'd forgotten that Lance and Bella dated back in high school. That was about a million years ago."

"Nah, only thirty," my dad said. "But a whole lot has changed since then, hasn't it?"

I blinked and leaned in closer. It was hard to believe that Bella and Babbage were ever that young, but sure enough, here was the proof. They both looked so . . . thin.

"What was Darrel looking for?" my mom asked.

"A taillight for his pickup truck," my dad said dejectedly.

I was still trying to process this new twist. Bella and Babbage *did* have a history together. Maybe that's why Bella seemed so awkward when we brought up the ducks in Babbage's yard. What if their relationship hadn't ended well? What if they were bitter enemies? Was this her motive?

"That's exactly the kind of thing he could get at the

Conquistador," my dad continued. "The best I could do for him was to sell him a roll of duct tape to patch up the broken glass on the rear of his pickup."

My mom put a hand on my dad's shoulder. "We'll be okay, Jerry."

He smiled back at her. "No, Denise, we're going to be better than okay. We're going to be the wieners. Right, Paul?"

I looked up, startled back to attention. "Wait—what did you say?"

"We're going to be the wieners?"

"No. Before that. About Darrel Sullivan."

"Oh, that he had a busted taillight on his truck and the only thing I could do for him was to sell him some duct tape. But let's not dwell on the sad stuff. After all, we've got the Bellwood Bratwurst Bonanza to prepare for! The competition is this Saturday, and today is already Thursday, and so . . . Hey! Where are you going, Paul?"

I was already speeding toward the door. "Sorry," I called back, "but I just remembered a . . . joke . . . that I have to tell Peephole and Shanks!" It was a lame reason to leave so quickly, but I wasn't about to tell them why I actually needed to go: to set up surveillance on Darrel Sullivan, our new prime suspect for the storage shed break-in. "Um . . . can I go out for a little while?"

"That lawn isn't going to mow itself," my dad said sternly.

"Oh, go ahead, Paul," my mom interjected. "Just be home for supper. We're having bratwurst!"

A Loyal Customer

Peephole looked through the binoculars anxiously. "So when Darrel Sullivan comes out of his house, do we run over and tackle him? Because I'm not a great tackler."

The One and Onlys were in a strategic-surveillance position behind a big tree across the street from Darrel Sullivan's house. The binoculars weren't really necessary—we were close enough to see everything just fine without them. But they made the mission feel more official.

Darrel Sullivan's place wasn't hard to find: my dad had mentioned that he lived on Radford Street, near Honest Hardware, and his was the most conspicuous house on the block. The front lawn looked like a hurricane had collided with a yard sale. A rusty bicycle had been lying in the grass near the sidewalk long enough for weeds to sprout up through the spokes of the front wheel. Two semi-deflated basketballs were almost entirely buried by the overgrown grass, and a headless mannequin lounged against the front stoop. In the middle of the lawn was a kiddie pool filled with Ping-Pong balls next to a flock of plastic flamingos wearing tinfoil hats. One flamingo was leaning up against a hand-painted sign that read ALIENS! TAKE ME HOME! There were other signs, too. One read PRIVATE TENNIS LESSONS: INQUIRE WITHIN, with a spray-painted slash through it. Another said CHEAP LEGAL ADVICE FROM AN ATTORNEY-AT-LAW. The last line of the sign had been crossed out, too, and replaced with LAW ENTHUSIAST.

Finally, the dead giveaway: a green beaten-down old pickup truck with a duct-taped right rear taillight was parked at an odd angle in the driveway. A canvas cloth was draped over the bed of the truck, hiding whatever was below it from view.

"No, we don't just *tackle* him," Shanks whispered through a mouthful of cheese puffs. She had insisted that we bring "surveillance snacks," especially if it might turn into a lengthy stakeout, but she had dug into the cheese puffs as soon as we arrived. "We have to watch him first to make sure he's our guy. Once we get evidence, *then* we tackle him."

"We *have* evidence," Peephole argued, pointing at the pickup. "That's the same green color as the paint at the storage shed, and he's got a broken taillight! What else do we need? He's our guy! Maybe Darrel and Babbage have a history. What if he's always been jealous of Babbage's talent for cooking bratwurst?"

"Isn't everybody in Bellwood jealous of Babbage's bratwurst?" Shanks asked earnestly.

"Maybe we should hold off on the tackling," I suggested. "This case is getting more complicated by the hour. I just found out that Bella Tuff and Babbage dated in high school. I saw a picture of them together in my parents' old yearbook."

"Bella and Babbage?" Peephole made a face like he'd just taken a bite of chili-dog ice cream. "Is that even possible?"

"Of course it's possible," I said. "They're two human beings. They can date whoever they want."

"Yeah," he said, "but they're so . . . different."

"Well, they're obviously not dating anymore," Shanks said. "So maybe that's an important detail. But how does your old babysitter, Janice, fit into all of this?"

"Cahoots," Peephole muttered.

"Huh?"

"They're in *cahoots*," he said again. "Janice, Bella, Darrel Sullivan." He threw up his hands. "And probably Pocus, too!"

"Great," I said. "Now we're getting into conspiracy-theory territory. Let's scope out Darrel's place for a while. Maybe we'll see something that gives him away."

The minutes piled up. Helicopters flew by overhead. The occasional car drove by—and we'd squeeze out of view behind the tree. Surveillance could be pretty boring.

Peephole cleared his throat. "What I want to know is, do you think there are deer ticks in Bellwood?" He was crouching so that his butt wasn't actually touching the ground at the base of the tree we were using for cover.

"Entomophobia." Shanks drew out each syllable.

"Ento-what-now?" I said before popping a couple of cheese puffs into my mouth.

"It's the technical term for an irrational fear of bugs," Shanks explained. "And to answer your question: probably."

"My fear is not irrational," Peephole said. "You want me to name some tick-borne diseases? I could probably list ten off the top of my head."

"I wonder if your little sister is going to be like you," Shanks said.

"You mean, tall and smart and handsome?"

"No." Shanks kept squinting through the binoculars. "That is not what I mean."

Another few minutes of uneventful surveillance passed, accompanied by the constant crunch of Shanks's snacking.

"Maybe I should sign up to be a Junior Firefighter," Peephole said out of the blue.

"Really?" Shanks replied, turning to him in surprise. "You hate running, you're afraid of fire, and hoses remind you of enormous snakes."

"True," Peephole admitted. "But I like the shirts."

"You know," I said, "I have the strangest feeling that we missed something about the break-in at the shed."

"Like a clue?" Shanks asked.

I nodded. "Or a question, maybe. That we should have asked Portnoy. Or Byron."

"I have a question or two I'd like to ask your friend Janice," Peephole said.

"She's not my friend," I snapped, a little too defensively. I tried to make my tone more even. "I mean, she was my babysitter a long time ago. But I don't think she knew anything about the duckies. Last night she seemed as surprised by them as I was."

"Still," Peephole said. "Playing the tuba at midnight in the middle of the Bell Woods in front of a bunch of stolen ducks is . . . *kooky.*"

He wasn't wrong, but I didn't like what he was suggesting. "Kooky doesn't mean guilty," I said.

"Hey, Peephole, how about you go back in your memory and recite our conversations with Janice, Byron, and Portnoy at the storage shed," Shanks suggested.

"I remember everything I *see*, not everything I hear," Peephole said. "Which is lucky, because we have a lot of dumb conversations. Speaking of Byron, he seems like a pretty cool guy, don't you think?"

"You just like him because he's tall," Shanks said.

"You got something against tall people?" Peephole asked.

"Yeah," Shanks snapped, "they're too tall."

"Guys, let's focus on the mission," I said.

But Shanks kept egging Peephole on. "Hey, I forgot to tell you. I saw this old horror movie the other night where a lady gives birth to a half-baby, half-squirrel mutant. Maybe your sister will be like that."

"That's stupid," Peephole scoffed.

"No, actually, that was the plot twist. The mutant squirrel baby was a genius. She ended up saving the world from a nuclear war."

"Good for squirrel baby."

"Guys! *The mission!*" I said.

"What mission?" Shanks said with frustration in her voice. "We're just twiddling our thumbs here. Let's go take a look at the truck. Maybe there are more duckies under the cover."

Peephole and I looked at each other. Even he couldn't deny that we needed to take some kind of action. "All right," I said. "Here's the plan: I'll approach the eastern perimeter of Darrel Sullivan's house and creep along the driveway until I'm at the pickup. Shanks, you climb this tree to get a bird's-eye view of the neighborhood. If you see Darrel Sullivan coming back to his house, cry like a wounded crow. Peephole, you swing around the western perimeter of the house and make sure the backyard is clear while also checking for any clues. When you reach the driveway, I'll give you the hand signal to approach the truck. Okay?"

Shanks and Peephole looked at each other. "How about we just walk across the street and lift up the cover on his truck? I'm pretty sure he's not home," Peephole said.

Shanks bobbed her head in agreement.

"That works, too," I conceded. I guess my plan may have been a tad too complicated.

We sauntered across Radford Street as casually as we could and then walked straight up Darrel Sullivan's driveway toward his truck. Peephole and I swiveled our heads around wildly, making sure nobody was watching us, but Shanks kept her vision locked on to the cloth that was draped over the back of the pickup.

"If it's more duckies," I whispered as we reached the back bumper, "we call Portnoy immediately."

"Here goes nothing," Shanks said, reaching up to grasp the cloth.

"Car!" Peephole squawked as a green minivan glided past us down Radford. Shanks pulled her hand back, I looked at the sky, and Peephole actually shoved his hands in his pockets and started whistling.

When the van was safely out of view, Shanks took a deep breath and yanked the corner of the cloth up.

At the sight, Peephole emitted a terrified yawp, Shanks gasped, and I went still.

It was not the duckies that were under that cloth. It was a human foot. Attached to a hairy human leg. Presumably attached to a hairy human body.

"Oh my God," I eeked. "Darrel Sullivan is a *murderer!*"

"Let's get out of here!" Peephole cried, turning to run, but Shanks put a vicelike grip on his shoulder.

"We can't just run away! We have to see whose foot this

is. Come on!" In one fluid motion, she hoisted herself onto the bed of the truck and stood over the cloaked body. Peephole and I reluctantly did the same.

"Maybe he killed Babbage," I said, wincing as I looked down at the shape under the cloth. "We should call Portnoy."

"Maybe this *is* Portnoy," Shanks said ominously.

"Whoever it is," Peephole whimpered, "I'm not touching him."

Shanks clenched her jaw, bent down, and ripped the cloth away.

A fully clothed body of a man lay on the pickup bed, eyes closed, and head tilted slightly to the side. A spiky shag of black hair shot like a fountain from the man's scalp, and a bleached white goatee jutted from his chin.

It was Darrel Sullivan himself!

"Is he dead?" Peephole whispered.

"Hard to tell," Shanks answered.

"Uh . . . Mr. Sullivan?" I said tentatively.

No response.

"Somebody poke him," Shanks said, followed immediately by "Not it!"

"Not it!" I spat.

Peephole started to protest, but he knew he couldn't argue with the rules. He was it.

He took a deep breath to gather his courage, then bent over and stuck a finger directly into Darrel Sullivan's left eye.

"GAHHH!" Darrel Sullivan cried, sitting bolt upright and grasping at his face with both hands.

"Peephole!" Shanks said. "I meant poke him in the tummy, not the eyeball!"

"At least we know he's not dead!" Peephole shot back defensively.

"We wanted to *test* if he was dead, not kill him ourselves!"

"Well, I was it, and I could choose how I wanted to poke him."

"Guys! Quit arguing!" I barked.

"Who the heck are you?" Darrel Sullivan was looking up at us through his one good eye. "And what the heck are you doing on my pickup? And why the heck did you just poke me in the eye?"

These were all reasonable questions. We hadn't come up with a plan for actually *talking* to Darrel Sullivan.

"What are *you* doing on your pickup?" Shanks said in a tough voice, but then she eased up a little. "And, uh, sorry about your eyeball."

"I was trying to sleep," he growled, tentatively removing his hand from his eye, which was a little red but didn't look too bad.

"Strange place for a nap," Peephole said.

Darrel Sullivan swung his gaze across all three of us. He still looked annoyed, but he also looked curious. "I'm sure there's a good reason why you kids are on my truck. . . ."

We didn't know what to say. So we didn't say anything.

"What did you say your names were?" he asked, probably concluding that he needed to start with an easier question.

"I'm Shanks," Shanks said boldly.

Peephole pointed to his chest. "Peephole."

"And I'm . . . Paul," I said.

"That's it?" Darrel Sullivan asked, clearly unimpressed by my answer.

"I just don't have a nickname. *Yet*," I added defiantly. "So . . . how come you're sleeping in your pickup truck?"

"If you must know, I've got a lobster problem inside my house," he said.

"A what?"

"A lobster problem. As in: several vengeful lobsters that are really good at hiding. I was working on a dish for the Bratwurst Bonanza and things went awry, and now I can't go to sleep without getting pinched by a crustacean who resents being considered part of lunch. For the last couple of days the truck has been more comfortable. That is, until you three showed up."

"Yeah," Peephole said. "Apologies for that. I figured you were dead."

"In the habit of poking dead people's eyes out, are you? Now, what was it you kids wanted again? I hope it's not tennis lessons, because I think a lobster pinched a hole in my racket."

The three of us looked at each other, unsure of where to begin. "We have some questions for you," I started cautiously. "See, we've been sort of investigating this thing—"

"Why did you steal the duckies from the police shed and dump them in a swamp in the Bell Woods?" Shanks blurted.

Darrel Sullivan looked surprised by the question, even taken aback by it. "A swamp?" he said.

"You heard me," Shanks said. She could be stone-cold when she wanted to be.

He scooted himself back up against the side of the truck bed, ran a hand through his hair, and gingerly rubbed his eye. He blinked a few times and silently studied us. "I don't know anything about a swamp."

Of course he would deny it, but his reaction seemed kind of weird to me. It was the mention of a swamp that confused him, not the duckies or the theft. I decided to go out on a limb and ask him about it. "How come you said 'a swamp' instead of 'the duckies' or 'the police shed'?"

I thought I detected a moment of uncertainty in his face, but he composed himself. "The ducks from Lance Babbage's yard, right? Everybody knows about them. It's front-page weirdness. What kinds of questions are these, anyway?" He tilted his head at me. "Are you kids, like, playing detectives or something?"

"We're not playing," Peephole replied, trying to hide the tremble in his voice. "We *are* detectives."

Darrel Sullivan gave a mocking chuckle and stroked the thick strands of his white goatee. "Okay, kiddos, if that was all you wanted to ask me about, I've got some things to do—"

"We know you stole the ducks." Shanks pressed on. "We're on the Bellwood Police Junior Detective Force. We examined the crime scene and found evidence linking you to the break-in. Now spill the beans."

She may have been small, but, man, could she be fierce.

Darrel Sullivan chuckled again, but this time it sounded hollow. "Evidence? Like what?"

"Your tire tracks are all over the scene of the crime," Shanks said. "And then there's your busted taillight. And I bet if we examined your truck, we'd find a little bit of the green paint scratched away."

He swallowed hard and narrowed his eyes at us, as if trying to remember something. "That's it? There are probably a hundred busted taillights in Bellwood. Not much to go on there."

"The jig is up, Sullivan!" Shanks was almost shouting. "You put the duckies in Babbage's yard, and then you broke into the police shed so you could dump them in the Bell Woods. . . ."

Listening to her, I couldn't help but think about how ridiculous the whole thing sounded. But she had a full head of steam.

"... and let me tell you another thing, buster, no amount of crazy head games and murdered lobsters will help you beat Babbage at the Triple B, so just confess already!"

Darrel Sullivan stared at her, his mouth slightly open. His eyebrows were perked up a little, as if he found us all mildly amusing but was already getting a little bored.

"Okay, kids," he said, rubbing his eye again. "Now, this has been a real blast, but I'm afraid it's time for you to run along."

We were at a standstill. We'd slammed down our full suspicion in front of Darrel Sullivan, but he was stonewalling us. It wasn't like we could *make* him confess.

"B-b-but," Shanks sputtered, not willing to end the interrogation without a full confession.

Peephole, however, was already easing himself down off the truck bed. I, too, was about to turn and go, when I noticed a small patch on Darrel Sullivan's shirt. I squinted to read the little red letters: DUNNING TOY COMPANY.

That was the company that made the rubber duckies!

"You work for Dunning Toy Company?" I asked, trying to sound as casual as possible.

Darrel Sullivan's face registered confusion and mild alarm, but then he looked down at the patch on his shirt and relaxed. "That's right, kid. But don't get excited—I'm just a delivery driver."

An idea came to me. "We know about Schuylerville Lake," I said boldly.

He whipped his face up to me, raw shock in his eyes. "How could you know about that?"

"We have our sources," Shanks said, playing along.

Darrel Sullivan went pale, and a thin bead of sweat trickled down from his forehead. "You kids called the police?" His voice had lost all of its confidence. In fact, he sounded downright panicked.

"Yeah, we called the—wait, what?" Shanks said, her voice switching from tough to confused in midsentence.

The sound of a car door shutting drew our attention to the street. We turned our heads to see Officer Portnoy walking across the lawn toward us, an expression of disbelief on his face. That expression didn't last long, though, because he tripped over one of the deflated basketballs and caught himself just before falling on his face.

Darrel Sullivan stood up and pointed to us, then shouted to Portnoy. "You've got to call your junior detectives off! They're questioning me for no reason. I'm a law-abiding citizen. I know my rights!"

Portnoy stood at the foot of the pickup truck and considered the scene. "Junior detectives, huh?" he said. He seemed confused and annoyed at our presence, but he didn't bat an eyelash at the giant lobster that had just wandered from the front porch and was now pinching his pant leg.

"I don't know what passes for law enforcement in this town anymore," Darrel Sullivan said, "but if you want to ask me questions, why'd you send the munchkin patrol?"

Portnoy's mustache seemed to turn a shade darker. "First of all, there're no such things as junior detectives. And second, I didn't come here to question you. I happened to be driving down Radford when I noticed some litter on the side of the road. Somebody left a bag of cheese puffs on the sidewalk. I pulled over to pick it up and noticed you three kids"—he pointed at us—"standing on the bed of a pickup truck."

"Litterers." Peephole stuck his chin up. "Is there anybody worse?"

"I can think of a few things worse," Portnoy replied. "Now, Macaroni, I think it's time you and your friends went home. . . . Mr. Sullivan"—here he touched the brim of his police hat—"I apologize for the inconvenience, and I wish you a pleasant afternoon."

He turned and started walking back down the driveway, shaking the lobster free from his pant leg. I noticed that he stole a quick glance at the truck's broken taillight.

Shanks looked like she was about to argue, but I threw my hand over her mouth and ushered her off the truck bed. Portnoy looked like a volcano that was seriously considering blowing its top, and I wasn't interested in sticking around until that happened.

"Hey, kids," Portnoy said, before we could get away.

"Yes, chief?" Peephole answered.

Portnoy seemed to wince. "The next time I have to remind you that there's no Bellwood Police Junior Detective

Force, it'll be at the police station. With your parents. Understand?"

We nodded. If the One and Onlys were going to continue this investigation, it would have to be a covert operation.

It was a good thing we had so much practice at being sneaky.

⇒ 12 ⇐

Yay, Mud!

The tall trees lining the old forest road didn't look so scary in the daylight. In fact, they looked pretty darn normal.

Leading the One and Onlys into the Bell Woods, toward the swamp where the duckies were dumped, I remembered the way the trees had been silhouetted in the darkness the night before, how their thin branches had spidered out at me like some otherworldly Goliaths as I followed the wavering headlight of Janice Wagner's scooter. I remembered how spooked I'd been.

But now the Bell Woods seemed so ordinary. *And that's Bellwood in a nutshell,* I thought to myself. *Mundane at first glance, but totally bizarre once you look underneath.*

"Duckies!" Peephole hooted, standing up on his pedals and pointing at a yellow mass in the woods on our left. He lost his balance and nearly wiped out, but he grasped the handlebars just in time.

We veered off the forest road and rode into the clearing where the duckies were resting on a thick bed of mud. Unlike the Bell Woods, the duckies seemed just as eerie in the daylight as they had in the darkness the night before. Maybe even more so, because now I could see their wild little eyes peering in every direction.

"Tire tracks! Again!" Shanks said, pointing at the ground. "They lead from the road to the ducky pile. And look! There's a bunch of footprints, too. Yay, mud!"

We ditched our bikes and ran to get a closer look.

"Guys," Peephole said tensely, "I think whoever dumped these duckies has just been here."

"Why do you say that?" I asked, alarmed.

"Because these tracks are fresh." Peephole pointed a long, bony finger at the ground by his feet. "Like, *really* fresh."

"Let me see," Shanks said, bending down to inspect the tracks. Her face scrunched up for a second, and then her expression changed. She looked up at Peephole slowly.

"You're right. These footprints are fresh. Because they're yours."

Peephole stood up and turned around, studying the tracks while thoughtfully scratching his chin. "Oh . . . yeah," he said sheepishly.

"Well, *these* definitely aren't yours," I said, crouching down over a smattering of footprints that were only a little bit bigger than my own. "These must be Janice's prints from last night. See how they're facing different directions but all stay in this little area? She was dancing around a lot. I think she was practicing the victory song for the Triple B."

"And here are some more!" Shanks yelped. There was nothing that she liked more in the world than footprints. "But these are bigger." She measured the footprint from heel to toe with her hands, then held up her fingers for us to see. The distance from finger to finger looked about the length of a ruler. "And all these prints lead directly from the tire tracks to the duckies. I bet these are the tracks of the person who dumped the duckies. . . . Darrel Sullivan, maybe?"

"Maybe," I said.

"There're even more over here!" Peephole said from about twenty feet deeper into the woods. "These have got to be Janice Wagner's. They're the same size, and they follow the same pattern." He did a little twirl and hop. He was probably trying to imitate Janice's dance, but he looked more like a giraffe walking over hot coals.

"Are you sure?" I asked. I closed my eyes and tried to remember if Janice had moved to a different spot. As far as I could remember, she had stayed in one place.

"You know what's weird?" Peephole said. "There are no connecting footprints between this set and the set by you, Paul."

"Interesting," Shanks said, hurrying over to look. "But there's a single small-wheel track, like from a scooter. That means Janice has been here more than once."

I was about to object, but I suddenly remembered something from a few nights ago. "Guys!" I said excitedly. "I forgot all about this. On Tuesday night, after the duckies showed up in Babbage's yard, a loud screeching noise woke me up in the middle of the night. I saw a car careening down Munchaus Avenue that must have been driven by the thief, and it must have been right after they dumped the duckies in the swamp!"

"What kind of car was it? Was it Darrel Sullivan's truck?" Shanks asked.

"Maybe. I didn't get a good look." Just like at the police storage shed, I had a hunch that I was missing something about the car. I closed my eyes and tried to remember. I'd heard the noise and got out of bed. I ran to the window and looked out. All I could see were red taillights flying around the bend way down the road.

That was it! The taillights! *Two* red taillights!

"It couldn't have been Darrel Sullivan!" I protested. "He smashed his taillight at the storage shed, right? But this car had both its taillights intact!"

And then I remembered something else I saw that night.

"What is it?" Peephole asked, reading the trouble on my face.

"Well . . . I saw somebody else from my window, right after the car drove away. It was Janice Wagner. She looked like she was sneaking back into her house."

A silence settled on us.

"*Cahoots*," Peephole said finally. There was something in his voice that annoyed me. "I'm telling you, they're all in cahoots. Darrel Sullivan, Pocus, Bella Tuff, Janice. Cahoots."

"I don't think so," I said firmly. I tried to imagine Janice as the one responsible for this strangeness. Did she have a vendetta against Babbage that we didn't know about? It didn't make any sense. She was so nice, so caring, so *not* a criminal. Could she really have orchestrated the ducky invasion of Babbage's lawn, broken into the police storage shed to get the duckies back, and secretly dumped them in this swamp? No way. Once, while babysitting me years ago, she sat through an entire improvised tap-dance routine that I did to "The Wheels on the Bus." And she called me Pauly Sweet, which was my tap-dancing alter ego. And she clapped afterward. She *had* to be innocent. "I just don't think we have enough evidence to tell who was involved or not."

"Enough evidence?" Peephole said with disbelief. "Paul, you just said it couldn't have been Darrel, even though we know he broke into the storage shed to get the ducks. So who is the only other person who keeps popping up to do weird stuff at all the crime scenes? Janice Wagner! And who is the only other person who can drive and who has a ducky? Bella Tuff!"

"And, hey, didn't you say a screeching noise woke you

up?" Shanks chimed in. "Did you notice how bad Bella Tuff's car was screeching when we biked by her yesterday? She must have been the one who dumped the duckies here!"

"No way. It was a different kind of screech," I insisted. It *was* a different screech . . . wasn't it? I guess I couldn't really be sure.

"They're all in cahoots," Peephole repeated.

"Would you stop saying 'cahoots'?" I snapped, and even I was a little surprised by the venom in my voice.

"What are you so touchy about?" Peephole asked.

"I'm not touchy," I shot back, but I clearly was.

"How come you don't want to entertain the idea that Janice and Bella are involved?" Peephole asked, and it sounded more like an accusation than a question.

"Because . . ." I didn't know what to say. "Because . . . why would they? I mean, Janice doesn't have a motive."

"Not true," Peephole said, raising a finger. "She said at the storage shed that her parents were taking the Triple B really seriously this year. Maybe it's a family operation."

"Or maybe she's protecting somebody else," Shanks suggested.

"It can't be them," I said, but I didn't have any good reason why not. I was thinking, *Because if they are involved, then two people I've always trusted are actually liars and thieves. And I'm not ready to deal with that.*

Peephole put a hand on my shoulder. "You're too trusting, Paul. Face it, dude. Your friends are dirty."

I brushed his hand off and took a step back. "You know what your problem is? You don't trust anyone. You're paranoid, Peephole. This whole ducks thing is not a big town-wide conspiracy!"

"Easy, Paul," Shanks said, her voice soft but serious.

I was angry, but I wasn't entirely sure why. "And we're supposed to trust Peephole's detective work?" I snarled and turned to face him. "A minute ago you were pointing out your own footprints! Even with all these clues, you're totally clueless!"

"That's enough," Shanks stepped in between us.

But I couldn't stop myself. "You're scared of everything! A heck of a big brother you're going to be!"

As soon as the words came out of my mouth, I wanted to pull them back in and bury them. Peephole's face flushed a deep red, and his shoulders slumped. For a split second, it looked like he might cry. But then he composed himself and raised his chin into the air.

"Peephole—" I started, but his cell phone buzzed in his pocket at that exact moment. I flinched at the noise.

He reached down and cast a quick glance at the screen.

"I've got to go," he announced, his voice even but thin. I could tell he was trying to hold it together.

"I didn't mean—"

"Gotta go," he said quickly. He retrieved his bike and headed back to the forest road. "My dad says it's urgent."

"Peephole, wait!" I shouted, but he was already pedaling away.

⇒ 13 ⇐

Duty Calls

There was one thing on this earth that my dad simply could not tolerate: a half-mowed lawn. But that's exactly what he woke up to on Friday morning. After my blowup with Peephole, I had been so distracted by all the crazy stuff going on that I completely forgot to finish the job. So before he left for the hardware store, he gave me a list of chores as long as the Great Wall of China. He was going to be home early to prepare for the Triple B, which was now only a day away, and he expected *everything* to be crossed off that list by the time he returned. The door slamming behind him sounded like the pounding of a judge's gavel after the verdict has been read. It looked like I'd be doing hard time all day long. The ducky case was going to have to wait.

The den needed dusting. The mudroom needed to be

de-mudded. The bathroom needed mopping. After that, the handles needed to be polished. The handles to what? The handles to everything. Wash the car, dry the car, wax the car. Dust the den again. Vacuum the stairs. Scrub the bathtub. Oh, and wipe that look off your face.

Break for snack. The menu? Bratwurst.

Snack over. Get a ladder and clean out the gutters. Pull weeds in the garden. Vacuum the dog. Vacuum the dog? Apologize for vacuuming the dog.

At four o'clock my dad came home and surveyed my work. "Good," he said. "Next time you'll finish the job the first time round."

And that was the signal that my sentence was over. I ran up to my room, opened the window, and sat on my windowsill. Munchaus Avenue softly hummed with activity. I could hear laughter and music tinkling from the houses and front yards all along the block. It was the eve of the Triple B, after all, the biggest day of the Bellwoodian year, and everyone was in a festive mood.

From the windowsill I could see all the way down the road. White houses. Blue houses. Houses the color of reptile bellies with long metal lightning rods poking up from their roofs like bug antennae. In my head I said the names of the families who lived in them: The DeLuccos. The Bachrachs. The Jenkersons. Three houses down, the Singh family was playing a raucous game of Wiffle ball in their front yard. It seemed like all three generations were there, laughing and shouting. I watched as Mr. Singh pitched and the youngest daughter swung and the little white ball popped straight up and the whole family seemed to freeze, staring up in the air, waiting for the ball to come down.

I pulled my phone out to give Peephole a call. I owed him an apology, but I wasn't sure what to say, exactly. Yeah, Shanks and Peephole were always teasing each other, but what I had said was different. It was *mean*. And worst of all, it wasn't true. Peephole was a fraidy-cat, but that didn't mean he wasn't going to be a good big brother. He had lots of awesome qualities. He was a rock star at math. He could reach things on every top shelf. He was loyal.

Why did I get angry out at the swamp? It just seemed like this ducky case was getting so complicated. Was Peephole right? Were Bella and Janice not the good people I thought they were? Everywhere I looked, it seemed like Bellwood was changing, but I wasn't sure if I liked it or not.

I called, but Peephole didn't pick up.

I went back downstairs and popped into the kitchen to see how the Triple B planning was going. My parents were deep into a brainstorm session.

"There's too much butter," my mom insisted.

My dad was in a frenzy. "There can never be too much butter!"

"Lance never uses too much butter."

"Lance?" I stepped forward and peered into a big silver mixing bowl on the counter. Yellow slop.

"Mr. Babbage," my mom clarified. "I don't know what he's got up his sleeve this year, but I'm nervous."

My dad rubbed his jaw. "Lance is good. Darn good. But this is our year, Denise. Isn't that right, Paul?"

"Yep. Your year."

He reached out and pulled my mom and me close to him. "*Our* year."

"Oh, Jerry," my mom whispered. She ruffled my hair.

It was a weirdly gooey moment, until we smelled something burning and noticed that one of the dish towels had caught fire.

The smoke alarm went *weee weee weee*, my dad was jumping around and letting loose a string of curses that I won't repeat until I'm forty, and the house phone had suddenly begun to ring. The whole circus took about a minute to settle down. When it finally did, my mom picked up the phone.

"Hello? . . . Dwight! . . . I was wondering how you were— Oh . . . oh, my . . ."

Dwight was Peephole's dad. He didn't call our house too often. I didn't know why he was calling now, but judging by my mom's reaction, it wasn't good. She was silent, biting her lip, her eyes sharp with concern. My dad and I stopped what we were doing and watched her. A lump formed in my throat, which I tried to swallow.

Every ten seconds or so my mom would say "Oh, my" quietly, and then nod her head. This went on for several minutes, until finally her eyes rested on me.

"I will, Dwight. Don't worry. . . . We'll find him. . . . Absolutely. . . . And Dwight? . . . congratulations." She hung up. "That was Alexander's dad," she said, looking at me with worried eyes.

"What did he say?" my dad and I asked at the same time.

She sighed. "Alexander's mother had the baby last night."

"What?" I blurted. "But Peephole's not supposed to be a big brother until the end of the summer."

"It was . . . ," she started, carefully choosing her words, "a difficult birth. See, honey, normally women are pregnant for forty weeks or so before they give birth. Alexander's mom is a little older than most moms, and that means there is a higher risk of complications. Thirty-two weeks is early. The baby is very premature."

"What does that mean?" I asked, hearing panic in my voice.

"It means that she's smaller than most babies."

"How small?"

"Well, you weighed eight pounds, nine ounces when you were born. Alexander's little sister is not even four pounds. Because she's so small, she needs help to do certain things."

"Like what?" I asked.

"Like eat." She paused, shifting her eyes to my dad. "And breathe. She'll be staying in the hospital for a while, hooked up to machines that will help her get bigger and stronger."

"But she'll be okay, right?"

"Of course she will," my mom said. But then she added, "We hope so. Paul? Have you spoken to Alexander recently?"

I cringed at the question, remembering the last thing I said to him yesterday. "Not today. And he's not answering his phone."

My mom bit her lip again. "I don't want you to get worried, honey . . . but he seems to have . . . wandered away."

"Wandered away?" my dad asked.

"He was with his mom and dad all night and day, but Dwight lost track of him a couple of hours ago. It's all so emotional," my mom said in a soft tone, but I could tell she was worried. "It's a lot for poor Alexander to handle right now. Dwight thinks he might have gone off for some time to think, but it's been quite a while. He's not answering his phone. And they've searched, but he doesn't seem to be in the hospital anywhere."

"Peephole is . . . missing?" I said.

"Honey," my mom said gently, "do you have any idea where he might have gone? Think. . . . Is there a place that he would go . . . to be alone?"

I didn't have to think long. I had a pretty good idea of where Peephole was. "Can I take my bike out and look for him?"

"Of course," my dad said. "Be careful, and take your phone."

On my way out the door, I called back to my mom. "What's her name? Peephole's sister?"

"Trillium," she answered. "So pretty. They named her after one of the earliest-blooming flowers of the spring."

I hopped on my bike, but before pedaling off, I took out my phone and texted Shanks.

Peephole's little sister is here and he's freaking out.
Biking to HQ now. Meet me there!

⇒ 14 ⇐

Waffle the Dolphin and the World's Tallest Man

Big trucks and construction equipment were parked all around the edges of the abandoned drive-in. Somebody had spray-painted the grass itself with various numbers and markings I didn't understand. A small mountain of rocks and dirt jutted up from one corner of the field, and the tiny sign that had previously given me chills was now enormous and bold and in color: THE CONQUISTADOR IS COMING!

The megastore looked like it was about to plop itself right on top of the One and Onlys' headquarters. Again, a cold tickle touched my spine, but I didn't have time to linger on it. I was here to find my friend. Peering across the field to the edge of the Bell Woods, I could see that I'd come to the right place.

Peephole was sitting outside the lean-to, hugging his legs, his back to me. His face was tilted upward at the

hand-carved ONE AND ONLYS sign that I'd made for our secret headquarters. As I pedaled toward him, dodging and
weaving around the churned-up landscape, I could see that
he was rocking gently back and forth.

My bike clicked to a stop at the lean-to, and I silently
took a seat on the ground across from him. He kept his
gaze fixed on the sign for a few seconds more, then looked
at me. His eyes were glassy and red. I wanted to ask him a
million questions. *What does Trillium look like? How is your
mom doing? Why did you run away?* I wanted to say something to make him feel better. To promise him that Trillium would grow bigger and get healthy. To tell him not to
worry about it. To let him know that I was there for him.
To apologize for being a huge jerk the day before.

But I didn't know how to say any of that stuff.

"We might need to make a new sign," I said instead,
"now that Trillium has arrived."

Peephole sniffled and dragged the back of his hand
across his nose. He turned and looked at the field. "What's
the point? Pretty soon we won't have a headquarters. This
will all be a parking lot for the Conquistador."

His tone was sharp, but his voice was weak, like he could
break and float away at any moment. I wondered if he was
right about our headquarters, but that was a question for
later. Right now I had a best friend to talk to. And it looked
like I wasn't going to have to do it alone.

Shanks wheeled up, dismounted, and stood in front of

Peephole, all in one swift motion. He looked up at her, and his expression seemed almost scared about what she might say. She crossed her arms, tilted her head, and gave him a hard look. Even I wasn't sure what she was going to do. These two had their history, and they didn't always see eye to eye.

Shanks stepped forward, leaned down, and gave Peephole a bear hug around the neck. I guess you don't always have to speak to say the right thing.

"Your parents are flipping out," she said after finally letting go.

"I know." Peephole rubbed his eyes. "I should call them."

"You should," Shanks agreed. "But first, we want to hear about your little sister. Is she half-squirrel, like I guessed?"

Peephole cracked a slight smile and flicked his eyes up at Shanks and then at me. "Trill is all human. She's so small and pink." He cupped his hands like he was trying to catch water dripping from a faucet. "She could fit right in my hands. I've never seen anything so . . . fragile."

I tried to imagine what Trill must look like. Four pounds seemed too light for a person, even for a baby. Could she really fit in the palm of Peephole's hand? Would she ever be tall and lanky like her older brother?

"She's hooked up to this machine," he continued. "It's called a CPAP. It helps her breathe. And there are a few other babies in the same room with her. It's like something out of a science-fiction movie. Tiny people everywhere, hooked up to tubes and computers that are always beeping. Nobody pays attention to most of the beeps. Like a parking lot full of cars and everybody's alarm is going off and nobody cares. But every once in a while, there's a particular kind of beep, more like a ringing, and then all the nurses and doctors rush over to see."

"Sounds kind of scary," I said.

Peephole shifted on the grass. "It is, I guess."

"But what happens if Trill's machine is ringing but nobody hears it? What if all the doctors are looking after another baby, and they forget about Trill?" As soon as I asked this, I knew that it was a mistake. Peephole's face said that he'd been worrying about the same thing. I had only managed to make him more nervous.

"All I know is," he said slowly, "you have to breathe to live."

It didn't seem fair. The Calloways were nice people. So what if Mrs. Calloway was a little bit older? She was always smiling. Always saying nice things to everybody. Didn't that count for something?

All I could think about was how gigantically, monumentally, astronomically lucky I was. To have both of my parents. To have such good friends. It wasn't a thought I'd ever had before. But it wasn't really a thought at all. It was more like a feeling. Kind of a wave of gratitude, I guess.

Peephole broke the silence. "I always thought that

everybody would be happy." He was squinting across the field at the old drive-in screen. "Things have been so hard on my mom these past few weeks and . . . I *want* to help. I just don't know how. I figured that as soon as the baby came, things would be easier. I know that babies are a lot of hard work, but at least people would feel better, you know? Maybe there would be some kind of celebration." He shook his head. "But everybody is so nervous and exhausted. My mom and dad whisper everything they say. It's like we're all too worried to be happy yet. And there's nothing I can do about it." He wiped his eyes. "Being useless sucks."

"Trill is going to be okay," Shanks said. "And you're not useless. We're in the middle of a big case, remember? *We* need you." She sounded so certain that it gave me a moment's relief. Shanks had this strange power: sometimes when she said things, you couldn't help but believe her.

But Peephole didn't look convinced. "For what?"

"Because . . . ," I said, but then I paused. The words weren't coming.

Peephole's red-rimmed eyes met mine. There was a tiny bead of snot trickling from his nose, but this wasn't the time to mention it.

". . . because we're not the One and Onlys without you," I said.

He blinked and wiped the snot from his nose. Finally, he nodded.

"You know," Shanks said, her voice perking up, "this

whole thing reminds me of Waffle the Dolphin and the world's tallest man."

"Waffle the what?"

"Waffle the Famous Dolphin."

"If he's so famous, how come I've never heard of him?" Peephole asked.

"Her," Shanks said. "Because this happened a while ago, and in another part of the world. As I was saying, everybody loved Waffle the Dolphin. People would come from miles around to see her perform her tricks. But one day Waffle the Dolphin didn't perform any of her tricks. Something was wrong with her. She didn't have any energy, and she kept making this I'm-a-dolphin-and-I'm-in-pain noise. So they called in all the leading dolphin doctors, but none of—"

"Dolphin doctors?" I asked.

Shanks ignored my interruption. "None of them could figure out what was wrong with Waffle. Finally, one doctor noticed something: there were chunks of plastic scratched away from the sides of her tank. The doctor guessed that Waffle had swallowed a bunch of the plastic, and that was what had made her sick!"

"That's stupid. Why would she eat a bunch of plastic?" Peephole said. He seemed annoyed, which was a great sign. He was coming back to life.

"Asks the guy who once chugged so much lake water that he barfed," Shanks responded.

I snorted a laugh, and even Peephole grinned.

"Anyway," Shanks went on, "they tried everything they could to get the plastic out of Waffle's stomach. The leading dolphin doctors said that surgery would be too risky. They tried to make Waffle barf, but she wouldn't. They even created a long metal arm to reach into Waffle's mouth and down to her stomach to grab the plastic, but Waffle's throat kept clamping up as soon as she felt the cold metal. They realized what needed to happen. Somebody had to reach with their own arm into Waffle's stomach and grab all the bad stuff."

"So did it work?" I asked.

"Well, yes and no. It turns out they were right—Waffle's throat didn't close up at the touch of a human arm. But there was a problem. Nobody's arm was long enough to reach all the way into her stomach. So they did the most logical thing they could think of: called the world's tallest man and asked for his help."

Peephole was doubtful. "How do you come up with this stuff?"

"I *didn't* come up with it. There is truth in every story I tell! Now, where was I? Oh, yeah—they called up the world's tallest man, who lived alone in a hut up in the mountains. He'd moved there a long time ago because he was tired of all the attention he got for being so tall. People liked to take their picture with him, but nobody *needed* him. But when he heard about how sick Waffle was, he knew that this was his chance to make a difference. So he hiked down from the mountains, which took him about three days."

"Couldn't fit in a cab, I suppose," Peephole said.

Shanks flashed him a look, then continued the story. "By the time he got to Waffle the Dolphin, she was in real bad shape. Everybody was worried that she was going to die. The world's tallest man took a long look at Waffle, then asked for a tall glass of water."

"The world's tallest glass of water?" I asked.

"Did he pour it on his arm?" Peephole asked.

"Did he pour it down Waffle's throat?" I asked.

"No. He drank it," Shanks said. "You'd be thirsty, too, if you hiked for three days straight. So after he finished his glass of water, which was tall but not the world's tallest, he rolled up his sleeve and crouched next to Waffle. He leaned close to her and asked if it would be all right if he reached into her tummy to get the harmful stuff out. Waffle said yes."

"I wonder about your definition of 'truth,'" Peephole said.

"I don't mean *out loud*. That would be ridiculous! She said yes telepathically. So the world's tallest man carefully reached into her mouth, down her throat, and into her stomach, and then he gathered up all the sharp little pieces of plastic and brought them back out. And guess what?"

"*That's* when she barfed," Peephole said.

I couldn't help but laugh.

"Waffle was immediately better," Shanks said, ignoring Peephole's comment. "She started doing all her tricks: flipping, spitting water, shaking fins. The world's tallest man had saved the day!"

"That's an incredible story," I said. "So the point is, even when a situation seems hopeless, there's always a solution? And you never know when you might be called upon to help?"

"Point?" Shanks shrugged. "Beats me. I just thought Waffle was a funny name for a dolphin."

Classic Shanks.

A clanging sound arose from the field, sending up a flutter of birds from a nearby tree. We turned to watch a pair of construction workers in yellow hard hats swinging sledgehammers at the metal base of the old drive-in screen. It was just a matter of time before that piece of Bellwood's past was torn down forever.

I imagined everyone in Bellwood gathering outside the Conquistador's front doors at the end of the summer, waiting for them to yawn open, and then all of us feeding ourselves to it at once.

"It's been a crazy week, huh?" I said.

"You're telling me," Peephole agreed. "I feel like I can't make sense of anything."

"Don't worry," Shanks said. "You'll figure out how to be a big brother one day at a time. And, by the way, you should probably call your parents. But now, can we try to make sense of the duckies case, please?"

"Good idea," I said. "Let's review what we know. First, the duckies showed up at Babbage's house on Tuesday morning. And nobody knows where they came from."

"Don't forget Tina Fish," Peephole said. "She was in Babbage's yard, too. And we *do* know where she came from—Schuylerville Lake. At least, that's what Bella Tuff says. But I'm not sure we can trust her. After all, she used to date Babbage back in high school, so she could have a vendetta against him. Maybe she's purposely leading us astray."

"Maybe we can trust her," I said but added, "and maybe we can't. But I think she's right about Tina. And what if the duckies were in Schuylerville Lake, too? But how would they get to Bellwood? And why Babbage's yard?"

"That's what we need to figure out," Shanks said. "Let's get back to the facts of the case. Babbage is convinced that Mr. Pocus put the duckies in his yard as a kind of weird mental roundhouse kick to screw him up for the Triple B. Mr. Pocus is the chief taster, but would he sabotage Babbage's efforts just to be able to give somebody else the sausage crown?"

"Pocus is pure evil," Peephole grumbled.

"Yeah, but if Pocus did it, then why did we find evidence of Darrel Sullivan's car at the police storage shed break-in?" I asked. "Darrel Sullivan is a shady dude, *and* he works for Dunning Toy Company, which is the company that made the duckies. There's got to be a connection!"

"True," Shanks admitted, "but Darrel Sullivan's truck didn't match the description you gave of the car fleeing the Bell Woods the night the duckies were dumped in the swamp . . ."

I *did* see two red taillights, not one.

". . . and you've seen Janice Wagner sneaking around late at night, including at the swamp with the duckies."

Shanks was right, and I couldn't deny it. But I remembered another clue. "There was a second set of footprints at the swamp," I reminded them. "Somebody with bigger feet than Janice was out there, and their tracks actually went from the pile of ducks to the tire tracks. Whoever that person was, they're definitely the ducky dumper."

"Those tracks could belong to any of our suspects except Janice," Shanks said.

But who? I didn't want to admit it, but Peephole's "cahoots" theory was beginning to make sense. I bit my fingernails and looked out into the Bell Woods. In the winter, when all the trees were bare and there was snow on the ground, it seemed like you could see forever into the forest. But now, when all the trees were leafy and the underbrush was thick, it was hard to see anything at all.

I sighed and looked back at the One and Onlys. "I meant what I said earlier, Peephole." I tried to keep my voice steady. "About the One and Onlys. We do need you.

This is the best case we've ever had, and we can't solve it without you."

Peephole blew his nose on his shirt sleeve. It sounded like somebody karate-chopping a goose. "Thanks, Paul. But you might have to. My parents are going to kill me when I get back to the hospital. Besides, Trillium needs her older brother by her side. You know what's funny? I almost forgot the Triple B was tomorrow. We'll probably be the only family in Bellwood who's not there."

"You're absolutely right, Peephole," Shanks said, her eyes wide with excitement. "Everybody in Bellwood will be at the Triple B!"

"So?" I said.

"*So* the person responsible for all the ducky shenanigans will probably be there, too. What other chance will we get to have *all* of our suspects in the same place? If we're ever going to solve the case, it's got to be tomorrow!"

"Yeah!" I said, swept up in Shanks's excitement. "But . . . how are we going to do that?"

"We need to get a full confession from the ducky thief."

"Or *thieves*," Peephole said. "But . . . how are we going to do *that*?"

Shanks pursed her lips and squinted up at the sky, as if the answer were written up there somewhere. "We need a telltale heart," she said at last.

"A what?"

"A telltale heart. It's from an old horror story by a guy

named Edgar Allan Poe. My parents used to read it to me before bed. See, in the story there's this lunatic who strangles an old man and then hides the body in his house. The lunatic thinks he's gotten away with it, but then the sound of the old man's beating heart, *thump thump thump*, drives him out of his mind and he ends up confessing everything."

"And your parents read this to you as a bedtime story? That explains a lot," Peephole said.

Shanks bit her lip and arched her eyebrow. "Yeah . . . it *is* a little weird, now that I think about it. Anyway, we need a telltale heart for our plan to work."

Just then I caught sight of Mister E, our ducky that Shanks had swiped from Mr. Babbage's yard. He was still perched on the roof of our lean-to.

"I've got it!" I said, suddenly struck with an idea. "What's better than a telltale heart?"

Shanks and Peephole looked at each other, then looked at me.

"A telltale ducky!"

A plan was quickly formulating in my head. The only problem was I couldn't tell if it was brilliant . . . or the dumbest idea ever.

Tomorrow, at the Triple B, we were going to find out.

≫ 15 ≪

Igor, Please Pass the Mustard

My parents were in the kitchen, dancing together in front of the stove to the oldies station they always kept the radio tuned to. I stood in the doorway and watched them for a minute or two.

They shimmied from side to side in unison, singing along with the radio. When they didn't know the words to a song, their voices got soft and mumbly, but when the chorus came around again and they knew the words, they got extra loud and *belted* it out. My mom was a good dancer, but my dad was . . . well . . . not exactly a ballerina. He had two dance moves: one was an off-balance foot-shuffle thing that went along with a circular hand motion that looked like he was about to fall off a ledge while simultaneously struggling to reel in a twenty-pound marlin, and the other was a panicky wiggle where his hands shot up and his knees wobbled as if they were made of rubber. I suspect that this is the exact movement people make if they wake up and find that their pajamas are on fire.

The pot on the stove bubbled and belched out a pungent odor that was a cross between ketchup and gym shoes. My mom and dad were so absorbed in their bratwurst experimentation and old-person dance-a-thon that they didn't notice me watching them.

That was the thing about being an only child. Sometimes, you felt like the center of the world, a celebrity with all the attention you could ever want. It could really drive a guy crazy. But when I wasn't the center of attention, I kind of missed it.

The song on the radio faded, but my parents kept dancing, as if they could hear the music in their heads, and that was all that mattered.

"What's up, guys?"

My mom swiveled and flashed me a startled look. White flour streaked her hair, which made her look like a grandma. For a moment, it was as if I was peering into the future. "Paul! There you are!"

She crossed the kitchen and wrapped me up in an embarrassingly tight hug. She asked about Peephole. I told her. She hugged me again, and this time, it looked like she might cry.

"I forgot to tell you, Paul," my dad interjected. "I almost stepped on a mattabuddy in the backyard today."

"What's a mattabuddy?"

"Nothing, buddy, what's-a-matta with you?" He ruptured into a giggle and turned to my mom for a high five, but she smiled at him crookedly.

A new song started up on the radio. A fast and gritty rock-and-roll tune with a wacky saxophone playing all kinds of insane notes. My dad launched into his twenty-pound-marlin dance, making the reeling motion at me so that I was the fish that chomped on the wrong worm. For some reason, there was a spaghetti noodle dangling from his ear.

"Bratwurst, bratwurst. For breakfast, lunch, and dinner . . . ," he bellowed. "Bratwurst, bratwurst. Please make us the winner!"

If there was a trophy for weirdest family in Bellwood, it would be no contest.

I chopped onions and celery into tiny cubes and listened while my dad explained the ins and outs of a good "currywurst" recipe.

"Now, this sauce is not the main character of our dish. It's more of a sidekick that *helps* the main character on the journey."

"So who's the main character?"

"The bratwurst wrapped in a pancake. But like a good sidekick, the sauce makes everything possible for the hero.

See, with 'currywurst,' everybody gets hung up on the spices," he said, pointing at me with a wooden stirring spoon. The noodle that had been dangling from his ear seemed to have migrated to the spoon. He was standing in the middle of the kitchen while my mom pirouetted around him on her way from the fridge back to the stove. "And don't get me wrong, Paul, the spices are important. You need your paprika, your pepper, your chili powder—"

"*Beep, beep!*" My mom, carrying a big steel pot of sloshing something or other, nudged my dad out of her way with her elbow.

"But the secret ingredient, the real magic element that sets a Marconi 'currywurst' apart . . ." My dad lowered his voice and leaned close to me, as if revealing the answer to an ancient mystery. He waved the wooden spoon like a sorcerer's wand, and the noodle moved back and forth in a frantic wiggle. "Is the brown sugar."

"Sugar?" I said. Of course, I already knew about the secret ingredient because my dad gave me this talk every year, but it was important to him. My parents made a different dish for each Bonanza, but the secret ingredient was always brown sugar. Some dads show their kids how to change the oil in a car or throw a good spitball. I got "currywurst" advice.

When I finished with the onions, my mom handed me a bunch of green grapes and instructed me to remove the peels from each one.

"Grapes?" I asked. "In a 'currywurst'?"

My mom put a hand on her hip and tilted her head. "Did the hunchback assistant Igor ever question the mad scientist's methods?"

"Uh . . . I'm guessing no?"

"That's right. He followed his orders and tried to stay out of the way of the lightning."

"Got it," I said. "You want me to peel grapes, I'll peel grapes."

For every few grapes I peeled, I'd pop one into my mouth. I was tempted to eat more than one at a time, but I knew better. Once, Peephole and I had a contest to see how many grapes we could fit in our mouths. Peephole fit nine, which made him the winner. Before he could celebrate, though, he inhaled a couple of them and started choking so hard that a grape shot out of his nose. I smiled at the memory, but then I thought of all those beeps coming from Trillium's machine in the hospital, and how helpless Peephole looked hugging his knees out at our headquarters.

My mom had a talent for reading my mind. She put down her spatula and squeezed my shoulder.

"She's going to be all right, Paul," she said.

"Who?"

"Trillium."

"Oh. I know." I said it quickly, but I realized that I *didn't* know.

Now my dad turned to me. My parents were smiling,

but only with their mouths. Their eyes looked worried and sad. It was a look I was seeing a lot of these days from the adults in my life. That's when I realized that neither of them really knew whether Trill was going to be okay.

"So where was Peephole hiding out?" My mom asked.

It was sort of a trick question. I didn't want to say "our secret headquarters," because then it wouldn't be secret anymore. But I didn't want to lie to my mom, either.

I settled on the sort-of truth. "Out at the old drive-in."

"It won't be the 'old drive-in' for long," my dad said. "By the end of the summer, that will be the Conquistador."

He was right, and I knew it. But I still didn't have to like it. That old field was where Bellwood used to gather on Friday nights to watch movies. Everybody there, together. It was where the One and Onlys met to solve mysteries. To tell stories. To talk nonsense. To comfort each other.

And now . . . the stakes with pink ribbons, the churned-up dirt, the rows of construction equipment. THE CONQUISTADOR IS COMING!

My dad seemed to read my thoughts. "Things are certainly going to change around here."

Change. That was something I was getting a little tired of. "But it won't change things for us, will it?"

My mom squeezed my shoulder again. "It might, Paul. See, a Conquistador opened up a couple of years ago in Lexington, and everybody started shopping there." Lexington was a few towns over from Bellwood. "The small stores, the local businesses—places like Honest Hardware—they just couldn't attract customers any longer. Those places lost a lot of money. Most have shut down."

"It's like a ghost town," my dad added, shaking his head. "All of Main Street is shuttered."

"How come Bellwood is letting the Conquistador in if everybody's so scared of it? And doesn't Old Man Shamtraw own that land? Why would he sell it to the Conquistador?"

"Scared?" Again, the defeated tone in my dad's voice. "Paul, they're *excited*. I don't know exactly why Mr. Shamtraw chose to sell the land, but I can guess. He probably made a lot of money from the deal. It's happening all over. Bellwood isn't alone."

I was afraid to ask the question that was on my mind, but I asked it anyway. "So what happens if we have to close the store?"

"We won't have to close the store," my mom said. "Not for a while, at least."

"If that happens," my dad said, "then we'll just have to make some changes."

There was that word again. "What kind of changes?"

"Well, I don't know yet, Paul. But your mom and I would need to find new jobs."

This was a totally strange thing to imagine. My parents had *always* worked at the hardware store. What else would they do? Drive school buses? Be waiters at a restaurant? Lawyers? Teachers? I couldn't picture it.

"And we might need to relocate." My mom uttered the words so softly that I wasn't sure I had heard her correctly.

"Relocate? What does that mean?"

"It means we would have to move, Paul."

Finally, I understood why my parents were afraid of the Conquistador. And for the first time, I realized how perfectly fitting the name "Conquistador" was.

"Unless . . . ," my dad started to say, then looked to my mom for permission to continue. She nodded. "Unless we win the Triple B. If that happens, then maybe . . . who knows? Maybe . . ." He looked too embarrassed to express the thought out loud.

"Maybe what?"

He finished the sentence. "Then maybe we could open up a bratwurst food cart."

I thought back over the past couple of weeks. The worried glances. The mumbled conversations. All that time spent in the kitchen, preparing. Now it all made sense.

It was anybody's Bonanza. But the Marconis *really* needed it to be ours.

"I just hope Mr. Pocus likes pancakes," my mom said, sprinkling a pinch of cinnamon into a mixing bowl. "Since he's the chief taster, our fate is in his hands."

"Ugh," I said. "I don't think Pocus likes *anything.*"

"He has turned into a bit of a grump in recent years," my dad agreed, stroking his beard.

"Recent years?" I said, taken aback. "You mean there was a time he *wasn't* a grump?"

As an answer, my dad held up a wait-a-sec finger, then dashed out of the room.

"Believe it or not," my mom said, "Mr. Pocus was a popular teacher a long time ago. Kids actually *wanted* to be in his class."

I fixed her with a sideways glance. I *didn't* believe it.

My dad bounded back into the kitchen with his yearbook once again. "Who would have thought I'd be unearthing this thing so much this week?" He laughed and flipped through the pages, then stopped on a photo collage near the back. "There!" He slapped a finger on a photograph of a smiling young couple holding paper plates. Both the man and the woman wore aprons, and the man had a smooth face with wide, kind-looking eyes. The woman was making a funny face with her tongue out and her eyes crossed.

"Who are these people?" I asked.

"Read the caption," my dad said.

Mr. Pocus, elementary school math teacher, and his wife, Clara, serve up their famous homemade tomato soup at the annual community picnic.

I blinked twice and squinted once again at the face of the young man. "Pocus was young once?"

"Funny how time works," my dad said.

"I didn't know he was married," I said, trying to make sense of Pocus's smile.

"Happily," my mom said. "In fact, I'd say he hasn't been quite the same since Clara passed about ten years ago. I think she was the one who brought him the most joy."

I kept staring at the picture, trying to process this new information. Of course, I knew that Pocus *had* to have been young at some point, but seeing a picture of him with his wife, smiling, having *fun*, made it real for the first time. Made *him* seem real.

"That's the smile we want to see tomorrow," my dad said, then twisted back around to sniff the boiling pot on the stove.

Ronald poked his nose into the kitchen, sniffing the floor, then looking up at us with raised eyebrows, as if surprised to find out that we were all still living in this house, too.

"You know who you're looking at, boy?" my dad said, pointing a goopy spatula at Ronald, who answered by slowly slurping a tongue across his snout.

"You're looking at the future wieners of Bellwood!"

⟩ 16 ⟨

The Triple B

Some of history's most important moments, in no particular order: the discovery of fire, the invention of the wheel, the French Revolution, the first steps on the moon, and the Bellwood Bratwurst Bonanza. I realize that as a Bellwoodian, I might be a little biased.

Ever since Wolfgang Munchaus threw the first Bonanza in an effort to save our little hamlet, Bellwood had never canceled a Triple B. And so it was an occasion for celebration when the town arose Saturday morning to a clear sky and fresh, breathable air. On the local news, reporters relayed the happy news that, thanks to the tireless efforts of regional firefighting organizations, the wildfire was now eighty percent contained. Crews had been digging containment trenches around the perimeter of the fire to make sure it couldn't spread, and the wind had shifted away from us. The fire hadn't been completely put out, but it seemed like the worst was over.

I woke up early and took a bike ride down the forest service road at the end of my block, into the Bell Woods. I needed to make a quick stop at the swamp to gather a backpackful of duckies. They were going to come in handy at the Triple B.

Even though my mom and dad had been dancing and laughing the night before, it was game time now. From the moment they woke up, they both wore focused, serious expressions on their faces and were buzzing around the house with purpose. My mom did a special yoga session, during which she bent into various contortions and chanted "Bo-nan-za" over and over again. Ronald and I watched this from the door while my dad stood silently with his hands in his pockets and stared at the empty space on the mantelpiece—the space he'd asked me to clear for the Triple B trophy.

Of course, I had big plans for the Triple B, too, but they didn't have anything to do with sausages. This was the day the One and Onlys were going to catch the ducky criminal. Well, at least two-thirds of the One and Onlys. I wished once again that Peephole would be able to help Shanks and me with my plan, but I knew he needed to be with his parents and Trill.

The Bonanza took place on the blacktop and playing field of the elementary school. On the car ride there, we listened to "Eye of the Tiger" twice. (We sat in the parking lot of the elementary school for a few extra minutes to hear the whole song the second time around—my mom danced with her shoulders and my dad snapped perfectly to the beat of a different song.)

As we unloaded the car, my mom ran through the list of supplies. "Spatula."

"Check," my dad responded.

"Grill."

"Check."

"Brown sugar."

"Check," my dad said, winking at me.

"Positive attitude."

After a moment of silence, I realized my parents were both looking at me, waiting for my response.

"Check about the positive attitude," I said.

"You feel that, Paul?" My dad held his hands at his sides, palms up, as if waiting for raindrops.

"No, what?"

"Triumph. It's in the air today. By the way, what do you have in there?" He pointed to my backpack.

I considered making something up, but why not tell the truth? "Rubber duckies."

My dad gave me a quizzical look but quickly changed his expression and flashed a thumbs-up.

There were rows of booths set up all over the blacktop,

and as we walked past them on our way to our designated booth, my parents sized up the competition. A lot of people in Bellwood entered the cook-off each year, but most of them just grilled up regular old bratwurst without trying for any kind of special flare or added ingredients. These people, my parents told me, never stood a chance. They were like the horses in a race that were fast but not fast enough to compete. Really, when it came down to it, there were only about ten or so teams that had a legitimate shot at winning the whole thing. But among them, as Chad Foster said, it was anybody's Bonanza.

Not everybody cooked bratwurst, of course. There were also booths featuring "notwurst" (the vegetarian version of the German sausage), sauerkraut, pretzels, funnel cakes, onion rings, ice cream, cookies, and elephant ears. Now, I'm no historian, but I'm pretty sure the French Revolution did not feature onion rings and elephant ears.

The Triple B wasn't just about stuffing your face, though. The playing field was home to all kinds of activities, games, and performances. I surveyed the scene around us. A man with white face paint and big red shoes (I hesitate to call him a clown because his curly blue wig was at his side and he was wearing a Metallica T-shirt) practiced making balloon wiener dogs. A woman with a top hat wobbled uneasily on six-foot-high stilts, bowing up and down with great formality. A cat with glitter in her fur ignored the repeated requests of her owner to do a flip, and as we passed by, the cat gave me a pleading look. An old man wearing lederhosen burped loudly and swung a chain of bratwurst links over his head like a lasso. A lady on a unicycle wobbled past. She was playing the *Star Wars* theme on a set of bagpipes, but she wasn't particularly good at it, or at unicycling. She nearly slammed into a table of sausage-themed jewelry, but she swerved at the last second, letting out a frantic wail from her bagpipes that sounded like a startled goat.

When we found our table, my parents and I got to work setting up. My mom propped up a hand-drawn sign that read TEAM MARCONI, with a cartoon bratwurst giving a thumbs-up. It was then that we all turned to see Mr. Babbage approach the table next to ours and start unloading his own cooking equipment. He was right next to us! I studied my parents, who were studying Mr. Babbage. They were grinning politely once again, but there was a kind of fascination and awe in their eyes, like the crowd outside the lion's cage at the zoo.

Babbage was wearing a very dapper outfit, as usual, but he looked especially gussied up for today's event. His black hair was expertly slicked to the side, his eyebrows arched upward like a camel's humps, and he wore a salmon-pink button-down shirt tucked into neatly pressed black slacks. His shoes were white and polished to a shine. He looked like the Emperor of Bratwurst. I tried to mentally compare him to the prom picture from my dad's yearbook, but the other Babbage seemed light-years away. Funny how time works.

I glanced down at my phone and saw that it was 9:55 a.m. In five minutes I was set to meet Shanks at the statue of Wolfgang Munchaus. "Ahem," I said, drawing my parents' attention back to me. "If there's nothing else you guys need, is it okay if I wander around and find Shanks and Peephole?" I could have added, *to set up a sting operation to expose the ducky mastermind*, but I thought it best to leave that part out.

"You know how this works," my mom said, turning to me. "The judges will come around and sample everyone's dish, and then they'll select five finalists to go onstage and present their bratwurst to Chief Taster Pocus."

Aside from being on the town council, the judges were all ordinary members of our community. Mrs. Schonfeld taught science in the high school, and her husband was an artist who made paintings of natural disasters. Mr. Bloom was a doctor. Mrs. Cavendish was an instructor at the driving school. The longest-serving judge was Mr. Quill, who sat in the park and ate croissants, getting flakes and crumbs all over his beard, muttering mild curses at the nearby birds. (This probably wasn't his day job, but I'd never seen him do anything else.)

The chief taster, on the other hand, was like the nine U.S. Supreme Court justices all wrapped in a single person. The "CT" was elected and held the office for a four-year term, and during the campaign before every election, candidates had to prove the prowess of their taste buds by performing various feats of flavor identification. Mr. Pocus was in his third term, which meant he'd been the CT my entire life. His taste buds were famous in Bellwood. The other 364 days of the year he was Mr. Pocus, terror of the elementary school. But on the day of the Bonanza, he was strictly Chief Taster Pocus, and nobody was more important. That was especially true for the Marconis this year. I thought about the Conquistador and the fate of Honest Hardware. I crossed my fingers and hoped that Pocus was in a smiling mood.

"If we make it through," my mom continued, "the final round begins at noon. Make sure you're back!" She insisted on a fist bump, and my dad gave me a two-fingered salute, then made me stick a name tag on my shirt that read TEAM MARCONI.

"Good luck, guys," I said, and turned to go, shifting my backpack of duckies from one shoulder to the other. "And good luck to us," I muttered to myself, because the One and Onlys were about to launch the dumbest (or most brilliant plan) ever concocted.

⇒ 17 ⇐

The Telltale Bath Toys

The bronze statue of Wolfgang Munchaus stood in front of the steps of the elementary school, grinning proudly out over the crowd of the 87th annual Bellwood Bratwurst Bonanza, a map in his left hand and a bratwurst in his right. I leaned against the base of the statue and surveyed the scene while I waited for Shanks. She was already five minutes late to our rendezvous.

The woman on stilts tromped up and down the aisles of booths, tipping her top hat at everybody. Kids were coming up to her and asking how come she was so tall, and one particularly little girl poked her foot to make sure she was real. A woman was trying to teach a man how to hula-hoop, and her movements were fluid and easy, like a thin plume of smoke, like she had been born hula-hooping. The man kept nodding and saying, "I got it, I got it," but the way the hoop kept on falling to his ankles proved he did not get it.

The glittery cat had a small crowd around it. It wasn't doing flips, exactly, but it was doing some kind of roly-poly movement that kind of resembled a flip. Maybe it was just trying to get all the glitter out of its hair. The cat's owner was clapping and cheering far more enthusiastically than any of the observers.

Suddenly, Shanks appeared at my side. She was holding a bouquet of electric-blue cotton candy. Wispy tufts of it were stuck to her upper lip, and it almost looked like she'd grown a sky-colored mustache.

"That's why you're late?" I asked, pointing to the cloud of sugar fluff.

She shrugged her shoulders. "Long line. Besides, I need brain snacks. We've got some serious detecting to do today." Her face momentarily disappeared behind the cotton candy, then reemerged with an even thicker blue mustache. She looked like a cross between Portnoy and a Smurf. "I just wish Peephole was here," she sighed. "Paul . . . are you worried about Trillium, too?"

"Yeah. But it feels like there's nothing we can do for them."

A distant growl caught my attention, and I turned my head to see a single line of trucks, like a giant metal centipede, scuttling its way through Bellwood. I knew exactly where they were headed: to the drive-in field. The ominous rumble represented the arrival of the Conquistador.

"We can do one thing for Peephole: solve the case," Shanks said. "You got the duckies?"

I took the backpack off my shoulder and opened it. The tiny little rubber eyes looked up at me like they were excited to help in our ruse. From a side pocket I took out two black markers.

"Let's go over the plan one more time," I said, passing Shanks a marker and an armful of duckies. "First, we tag all of our little yellow friends here with the word 'Confess' in bold letters, and then we scatter them all over the Triple B."

"Yeah!" Shanks chuckled, rubbing her hands together with delight. "And then we make a few special duckies for our suspects: Pocus, Bella Tuff, Janice, and Darrel Sullivan. We'll write, 'We know you did it! Your days of ducky mischief are over! Confess to the statue of Wolfgang Munchaus, you dastardly criminal mastermind!'"

I looked down at the little ducky in my hand. "I don't think that's all going to fit on here. How about we write, 'We know. Confess to Munchaus!'?"

"Okay, fine. But we gotta be extra-stealthy when we slip them the duckies. They can't see it was us!"

"Exactly. It'll be just like the telltale heart in that horror story your parents read to you. We'll set up our original ducky, Mister E, at Wolfgang's feet," I pointed to the bronze statue above us. "And then we'll wait. Eventually, whoever of our suspects is the true ducky thief will be driven mad by the sight of the duckies everywhere they turn, and soon they'll be so overwhelmed with guilt that they'll pour out their confession to us right here."

"And that's when we tackle them!" Shanks hooted, jabbing a fist into the air in front of her.

"What is it with you and tackling?" I asked.

"Sorry. Just excited for this."

Once the telltale duckies were all tagged, we cast ourselves into the thick of the Triple B crowd to lay our trap. We put duckies along contestant row, where the hopeful Bonanza entrants were eagerly serving their carefully prepared dishes. We put a ducky on the counter of Jojo's Fried Frog Legs food truck. We dropped two duckies on the ground near the Rodents of the Wild West booth, where you could get your picture taken with Billy the Echidna or Wild Bill Chipmunk. We put a ducky on the Bellwood Fire Department booth, where Byron was recruiting kids for the Junior Firefighters. We put a ducky on the hood of the Bratwurst Mobile, which was parked in the center of the field, with a ring of admirers around it. We scattered duckies around the cute-pet contest, causing a dustup between a pug and a Chihuahua. We put duckies in the Bellwood of the Past tent, sponsored by the Bellwood Historical Society, and we put duckies in the Bellwood of the Future tent, sponsored by the Bellwood Sci-Fi Society. Duckies, duckies, duckies.

Finally, we were left with our last four duckies, each with "We know. Confess to Munchaus!" scrawled on their backs.

"Now," I said, gripping a ducky and sweeping my eyes over the crowd, "we need to find our suspects."

"Pocus!" Shanks flung her pointer finger in the direction of a small clump of Bellwoodians gathered at the Pet-a-Llama booth. The booth was exactly what it sounds like—when it was your turn, you got to pet a real-life llama. The llama, whose name was Hal, stood there with a blank expression on his face while people stroked his furry head and back. He had a pink bow tied around his neck and some funny little gold booties on his feet and insanely long eyelashes that swooped upward like a wave. Pocus stood at the end of a long line, his hands folded patiently behind his back.

"Maybe the llama will bite his hand off," Shanks suggested.

"Shanks! That's a horrible thought," I scolded, but then I remembered a fractions quiz Mr. Pocus had given back to me. There was a mustard smudge on the top of the page, and he'd drawn an arrow to it and wrote, *Your grade.* As bad as that was, he was even meaner to Peephole. And then there was Byron Willis, who'd needed to take time off from school after having Pocus as a teacher. "Maybe just a finger or two."

Shanks snatched the ducky from my hand and trotted up behind Pocus, careful not to attract any attention. She rocked back and forth on her heels, pretending to casually take in the sights of the Bonanza, then leaned forward and slipped the ducky into Pocus's sweater vest pocket. With that, she disappeared back into the crowd, popping up at my side a few moments later.

The two of us watched from a safe distance, wondering when Pocus might discover our bait, but he never reached into his pocket. Finally, he made it to the front of the line. He stepped up next to Hal the llama, stared him in the face, and then gingerly tapped the top of Hal's head, like he was testing to see if a stove was still hot. Instead of stroking the llama, he just kept his hand there, like it was tired and he was resting it. Then, an odd change occurred in his expression. It reminded me of a wax statue melting in the sun.

"What's happening to Pocus's face?" Shanks asked, her eyes wide with bewilderment.

The only reason I knew the answer was because I'd seen Pocus make that face before—in the yearbook that my dad showed me from thirty years ago. "He's . . . *smiling.*"

It was a big-time smile, too. Wide and joyful. And then he leaned in and kissed the llama on the nose.

"Peephole would never believe what we just saw," I said, wishing once again that the One and Onlys were in full force. I wondered if he was at the hospital with his sister and mom, and hoped, once again, that everything was okay.

"I think Pocus might have lost his mind," Shanks said, her jaw still drooping.

"I think you might be right, and if he had anything to do with the duckies, we'll find out soon. But come on— we've got three more duckies to hand out, and either an elephant is giving birth or I hear a tuba nearby."

It was a tuba. Right around the corner of the elementary school, we found a cluster of kids clad in the official brown mustard–colored regalia of the Bellwood marching band. Chad Foster was there, trombone in hand, along with a short kid carrying a big drum, a slim girl with an accordion strapped to her chest, and Janice Wagner, standing next to an enormous tuba. I did a double take at Janice's instrument. It seemed to me that either Janice had shrunk or her tuba had gotten bigger. In fact, it was so big that a guy was helping her hold it up. This guy, who had thick-rimmed glasses and a haircut that made his head look like a bucket, seemed to be showing her how to play it. I recognized him as Mr. Mundo, the band teacher.

Janice practiced her movements, and unlike the night I saw her in the woods, she kept the tuba on the ground and twisted around it. Even though she wasn't able to twirl and hop like I'd seen her do before, I was hypnotized by her playing.

Chad Foster, who was in our grade, was also practicing his dance steps, but he was a lot less graceful than Janice. In fact, he looked like he was trying to keep his balance during an earthquake. Mr. Mundo glanced over at him and shook his head slowly.

"Come on, dude," Shanks said, suddenly appearing at my side though I hadn't noticed she'd left. She pulled me back into the human traffic of the Triple B.

"But we didn't give Janice a telltale ducky," I complained.

"I did. I put it on her scooter while you were zoning out," Shanks said in a slightly annoyed voice.

We knew that Darrel and Bella were both entering bratwurst dishes in the competition, so we zipped back over to contestant row on the other side of the blacktop. It didn't take long for us to find them both.

"They're right next to each other!" Shanks exclaimed.

A hand-scrawled sign on Darrel Sullivan's table announced his bratwurst and "lobster" rolls, and I was very curious about those quotation marks around "lobster." Darrel was grinning through his bleached white goatee as he handed out samples of his creation.

At the next table over, Bella served up her "Tuff's Troutwurst." I wondered if the fish on those plates had once been friends with Tina Fish, may she rest in peace.

"What's the plan?" I asked. "We can't just walk up and hand them the duckies. Bella knows me too well, and Peephole nearly poked Darrel Sullivan's eye out, so I don't think we're high on his list of favorite people."

"So we've got to put the duckies on their tables without them noticing us," Shanks replied.

We surveyed the situation, and it didn't look good. Both Darrel and Bella were facing out, so we couldn't sneak up from the front. Their backs were to the wall of the elementary school, so we couldn't sneak up behind them, either.

But then we caught a lucky break. A commotion from a few tables down the line caught everyone's attention. A man shrieked, a tablecloth came flying off, and a tiny furry thing came scampering up the pathway. Wild Bill Chipmunk, from the Rodents of the Wild West booth, had escaped and was making the most of his freedom run. Several frantic Bellwoodians chased after him, but he was a wily little guy, and he evaded his pursuers by darting this way and that, taking nibbles from every plate he passed. In an impressive leap, he bounded onto Darrel's table, knocking over the display, then jolted over to Bella's table, sending her carefully crafted dishes into disarray. Both Bella and Darrel sprang to their feet and joined the chase, bumping into each other when Wild Bill changed course.

"Now's our chance!" I squawked, and Shanks and I dashed over to their tables, placing a ducky on each of their chairs while they were distracted by the historical rodent.

"Back to the statue!" Shanks called.

We skittered through the Triple B, passing many of our carefully placed telltale duckies along the way. At the steps of the elementary school, we laid our final ducky, Mister E, at the bronze feet of Wolfgang Munchaus.

The first phase of the One and Onlys' most brilliant and/or dumbest plan was complete. And now it was time to wait.

Confessions

We waited. Leaning against the base of the Wolfgang Munchaus statue, Shanks and I watched the people of Bellwood pass by us like a babbling brook. Any minute, we figured, our guilty suspect would emerge from the crowd and confess everything. I hoped it wasn't Bella, or Janice, but I wasn't so sure anymore.

We waited some more. Any minute, we said.

Minutes passed. We kept waiting.

And then I noticed a man watching us. He had a blue baseball hat on and was wearing jeans and a jean jacket. In his hand was one of our rubber duckies, and he glanced down at it, then at us again.

"Who is that?" I whispered to Shanks.

"I don't know, but he's coming this way."

The man approached us cautiously, like we were wild

animals and he was on a safari. "Is this where I'm supposed to confess?" he asked.

"Uh . . . ," I faltered. Who was this guy? Could it be possible that the ducky thief was somebody who wasn't even on our radar?

"I found this," he said, holding up one of our telltale duckies. "And then I saw you kids here with another ducky, so I figured this must be the place."

"Yep," Shanks cut in. "You got something to confess?"

He sighed and nodded. "I've been wanting to get this off my chest for a while now. See . . . I'm the founder and president of the Bellwood Bigfoot Hunters Society, and . . ." He cast his eyes down to his feet. "And . . . well . . . I don't believe in Bigfoot." He looked up at us, instant relief on his face. He blew out a big breath and laughed. "I feel so much better! Thanks!" With that, he turned and skipped off into the crowd, looking lighter than air.

A minute later, a woman with short dark hair and a flowery dress approached the statue, a ducky in her hand. "I have a confession to make. I ate some plums that my husband was saving for breakfast. They weren't as delicious as I thought they'd be."

A few minutes after that, a man with long wavy hair confessed to eating all of his dinners in bed, then putting the dirty dishes in his bedside-dresser drawer because he was too lazy to take them downstairs to the kitchen sink. "It's my drawer of shame," he said.

"Maybe we should have been a little more specific about the whole 'confess' thing," Shanks said as the wavy-haired guy slunk into the crowd.

"Yeah," I sighed, and rubbed my neck. "I guess Bellwood's feeling a little guilty."

And that's when we saw him. Pocus. The ducky was in his hand. He seemed to float toward us out of the crowd, that odd expression still on his face. He was smiling. Not as wide and crazy as when he was with the llama, but the happiness was still visible on the surface.

"I've come to confess," Pocus announced to Mister E, and then he shifted his goofy grin to Shanks and me.

"You have?" I asked.

He nodded. "These duckies have changed my life. I've been seeing things differently ever since they showed up. Thanks to these guys"—he bounced the ducky in his palm—"I'm starting to have a little more fun."

"Fun?" Shanks repeated. "You are Mr. Pocus, right? The fourth-grade math teacher?"

Pocus chuckled. "I know, I know. I've been a bit cranky as of late."

That's the understatement of the year, I thought, but I kept my mouth shut.

"So," Shanks said, "you said you wanted to confess?"

Pocus closed his eyes and took a deep breath. "I confess that I lost sight of all the joy in the world. I've been difficult, I know." He pursed his lips. "Okay, I've been awful. A meanie. A jerk. A . . ."

"Butthead," Shanks said.

I flashed her a look, and Pocus raised his eyebrows in surprise. But then he broke into a chuckle. "A butthead, *heh-heh*. Yep. I admit that I haven't been the best version of myself in the last, oh, decade or so. But then I saw those duckies on Lance's lawn, and something about them made me pause. Maybe it was because there was no explanation for them."

"So . . . you don't know why the duckies were there?" I asked.

"Oh, I know exactly why they were there. But I didn't at first, of course. I was as baffled as everyone else. But then I realized that it was a message. From Clara."

Clara, I thought. Where had I heard that name? And then I remembered: the old picture in my dad's yearbook. "Clara was your wife."

Pocus nodded slowly. "The duckies are exactly the kind of thing she'd find funny. Because they don't make any sense at all. She would have gotten the biggest kick out of them. And that's why I know that, somehow, she's sending me a message from the other side. *Lighten up, Buttercup!*"

"Buttercup?" Shanks repeated.

"That's what she called me." Pocus laughed. "And then when my tomatoes were ripped up—"

"We didn't ruin your garden, we swear!" Shanks said, putting her hands up.

Pocus waved her off. "It doesn't matter who did it," he

said. "The only witnesses to that crime were my garden gnomes. And the truth is, I really don't care. In fact, I owe whoever did it a thank-you."

"You do?"

"You betcha. See, I've been holding on to those tomatoes for a long, long time. Clara and I used to grow them together. That was something we shared. We never had kids, and it sounds silly, I know . . . but the tomatoes were sort of our *children*. And for a long time after she died I protected them, worried over them. But I never enjoyed them. Did you know I haven't eaten a single tomato from my garden since Clara died? Can you believe that? All those tomatoes, gone to waste. I suppose in a strange way the tomatoes represented my memories of Clara. I was so scared to lose them. But when they were ripped up, it was like I had been cut loose from that weight. From that pain. I was given permission to move on. To grow something else. To start something new. And you know what I realized? My memories of Clara can never be taken away. They'll be with me forever, no matter what."

"Wow," I said, because nothing better came to mind. This was, of course, the same Mr. Pocus standing in front of us that we'd had for a teacher, but he looked like a completely different person. I saw, for the first time, that he was carrying so much with him. I had never thought of him as a real person at all, really.

"So you've got to tell me," Pocus said, leaning in closer.

"How'd you get all those duckies in Lance's yard without him seeing you?"

Shanks and I looked at each other, baffled. "But *we* didn't put the duckies in Babbage's yard!" I said.

Pocus tilted his head a little. "You didn't? Oh . . . I assumed it was you kids playing some kind of prank. So who *did* put the duckies there?"

"We don't know, exactly," I sighed.

"But we've got a few suspects," Shanks added.

"Well, that sounds like a good old-fashioned mystery." Pocus chuckled, then looked at the ducky in his hand. "Say, do you kids mind if I keep this? I think it'll be a good reminder for me. To relax. To have a little fun."

"Sure," I said.

"Thanks." He smiled at us, which still felt weird. "You know what I'm going to do first thing tomorrow morning? I'm going to plant a zucchini garden. And then I'm going to tear down that silly barrier between Lance's yard and mine. Life's too short for building walls." He winked at us, then turned and melted back into the scrum of bodies at the Bonanza. *There he goes*, I thought, *the meanest teacher in Bellwood*. But something told me that was about to change.

"Paul?"

My shock at Pocus's confession was interrupted by Bella Tuff, who was standing off to our side, watching us with a curious expression.

"Oh, hi, Bella." I suddenly felt very awkward.

Bella held up her telltale ducky. "What's this about?"

"I . . . well . . ." I looked to Shanks to take over, because she was usually the one who did all the tough talking, but she just stared right back at me. My face got hot, and my throat closed up a little. How could I confront a woman I'd known my whole life? "Bella . . . do you have . . . something to confess to us?"

Bella arched an eyebrow at me. "This has something to do with that fish you brought me, doesn't it?"

"Tina," Shanks said. "And the rubber ducky on your desk."

"I thought so," Bella said.

I worked up the courage to continue. "And . . . well . . . it seemed like you were . . . maybe . . . hiding something from us. About the day you missed work."

Bella shifted her footing a little, and she passed the ducky from one hand to the other. She didn't say anything. She seemed to be considering us. Maybe she was trying to decide how to respond.

"What are you kids, the police?" she asked, sounding more amused than worried.

"Junior police," Shanks said.

"Actually," I said, "we're amateur detectives. We're trying to get to the bottom of the duckies case."

"The ones from Lance's backyard?"

I nodded.

Bella took a couple of steps forward, a low rumble of a

laugh escaping her lips. "Well, you kids are perceptive. I'll give you that much."

"We are?" I asked, my voice squeaking. "I mean, we *are*."

"Yep. You caught me. I did lie about being sick that day."

"We thought so," Shanks said matter-of-factly. "Well, Peephole thought so, anyway."

"Well, can you blame me? Paul, I've known your dad for a long time. Jerry and I are good friends. But he's also my boss. After all, he does own the hardware store. And I couldn't very well admit to the boss's kid that I'd skipped work to go fishing."

"Fishing?" I echoed.

"That's right," Bella confessed. "I needed some fresh trout for my Triple B recipe, and Tuesday was the perfect day for fishing. I woke up, saw the weather report, and decided right then and there to head out to Schuylerville Lake. I told your dad that I'd come down with a virus. I felt bad for lying to him, but nothing's more important than fishing. Of course, I wasn't planning on *you* kids catching me in the lie."

That *did* explain why she acted so strange when Peephole asked her about her illness. But then I remembered something else. "But if you were out of town, then that means you couldn't have got that ducky you had on your desk from Babbage's yard. Where did it come from?"

"Strangely enough," Bella said, spreading her hands

out in a don't-ask-me-because-I-don't-know gesture, "I got that ducky from Schuylerville Lake. It floated right up to my boat when I was out there fishing. There were a few more just like it, but I picked up that one as a souvenir. How it got there? Your guess is as good as mine."

So the duckies *were* at Schuylerville Lake. But we weren't any closer to knowing *why*, or how they got to Babbage's yard.

"But what about your vendetta against Babbage?" Shanks asked. It didn't look like she was ready to entirely remove Bella from our suspect list. "We know that you used to date him in high school."

Bella's face softened. "Yup, Lance and I were together in high school. I daresay that we were in love, once upon a time. But vendetta? No way. I have nothing but fond memories of Lance. We had a great time together. In fact, I've been meaning to reconnect with him one of these days." She looked down at the ducky in her hand and smiled. "Maybe I'll take this opportunity to do that."

A moment passed during which nobody said anything. The sound of an accordion from somewhere in the festival reached our ears.

"I guess we owe you an apology," Shanks said. "Sorry we put you on our prime-suspect list."

Bella waved the comment away. "Nonsense," she said. "You're detectives. You've got to follow the clues. I wish I could help you crack the case, but it looks like you're back to where you started."

"Not exactly," I said.

With Pocus and Bella crossed off the list, we were down to two suspects: Darrel Sullivan and Janice.

19

More Confessions

We went back to waiting. More minutes passed as we leaned against the base of the Wolfgang Munchaus statue.

"This is stupid," Shanks finally said. "If Janice and Darrel Sullivan had been overwhelmed by guilt, they would have marched over here and confessed already. We've got to face it: they're not coming."

"You're probably right," I admitted. "So what do we do?"

"If they're not going to come to us," Shanks said, "let's go to them. I bet Darrel's still at his tasting table on contestant row."

Before I could argue, she was bolting through the crowded festival toward the tasting tables. I had no choice but to follow her, even though I was a little nervous to actually confront Darrel Sullivan. But I knew we had to do it. If we were going to solve this case at the Triple B, we had to take some risks.

Shanks was right: Darrel Sullivan was still at his booth, both feet up and resting unsettlingly close to one of his "lobster" roll plates. He was leaning back in his chair, which gave the impression that he was relaxed, though his shifting eyes told a different story. And I could see that under the table he was gripping our telltale ducky in his hand.

"So what's the plan?" I said.

"No plan," Shanks said, already marching toward him. "It's time to confront him."

She really was fearless. She stomped her way up to the table with such conviction that she almost seemed to be leaning forward. I'd made it to her side when she drew in a deep breath to let Darrel Sullivan have it.

"Okay, Sullivan," she began in her best junior police officer voice—but as soon as he noticed us standing there, he leapt to his feet, knocking over his chair, and sprinted away from us down contestant row.

Shanks and I stood there, rooted to the ground in disbelief. Then we snapped out of it. "He's fleeing!" I yelled. "Follow that goatee!"

The chase was on.

Darrel Sullivan weaved and bobbed through clumps of people, throwing backward glances at us at every turn. He didn't look particularly athletic, but he was surprisingly nimble. We did our best to keep up, but before we knew it, our suspect had made it to the edge of the crowded field, where it would be easy for him to blend in and make his escape.

He flicked one last look in our direction, and that's when we got lucky once again.

It was hard to tell who crashed into whom. The unicycle bagpiper lady wobbled in from Darrel Sullivan's right, a long, high, Scottish screech signaling that she'd lost control of her one-wheeled vehicle. The lady on the stilts, to his left, was *already* in midtumble, having just slipped on a discarded bratwurst bun. She yelped a quick "Look out below!" as the unicycle slammed into her stilts, causing a clattering, confusing, bagpipey collision. By the time Darrel turned back to see where he was going, it was too late. He was enveloped in the chaos, joining the heap of tangled bodies on the grass.

We caught up to him as he was sitting up. He rubbed his head and cast a ferocious look at us.

"You kids leave me alone," he snarled. "Every time you appear I get banged up. Your tall friend isn't here, so which one of you is going to poke my eye out today?"

"We're not here to poke your eye out," Shanks told him. "We want to ask you a couple of questions."

"I don't have anything to say to you."

"But how about to me?" The gruff voice came from behind us. We whirled around to see a familiar mustache.

"Officer Portnoy!" I exclaimed. "You were following Darrel Sullivan, too?"

"Nope," Portnoy said, shaking his head. "Actually, I was following *you two*. I saw you sneaking around the Bonanza earlier, placing those little rubber duckies everywhere. I could tell you were playing detectives again, so I've been keeping an eye on you. But I have to admit"—he turned his gaze on Darrel Sullivan—"I'm awfully curious as to why you were running away from our little friends here. I wonder"—he put a finger to his mustache—"if it has anything to do with the fact that we found traces of your pickup truck all over the scene of the police shed break-in."

Darrel Sullivan stared up at Portnoy for a long few seconds. His expression was hard. It seemed like he may have been considering another escape.

"Ah, what the heck," he finally said with a sigh, his shoulders drooping in defeat. "I guess there's no use in hiding it anymore. Yep, I broke into the storage shed. Drove over there late Tuesday night, around two in the morning, and smashed the lock with a bowling pin. I tried to steal the duckies, but I couldn't."

"Why not?" I asked.

"Because somebody beat me to it. They were already gone."

"Somebody stole the ducks *before* you? But who would do that?" Shanks asked.

Darrel Sullivan threw his hands up and let out a humorless chortle. "Ya got me. You're the detectives—you figure it out. All I know is, those duckies had flown."

"I still don't get it," I interjected. "Why'd you put the duckies in Babbage's yard to begin with?"

"The only thing I know about Lance Babbage is that he makes a mean bratwurst," he replied. "I didn't put the ducks in his yard." He looked beyond us out into the crowd, then ran his hand through his spiky hair. "Look, I'm as confused as you are."

"I think you better start from the beginning," Portnoy said.

"All right. The beginning. What have I got to lose?" He looked up at the sky and took a deep breath. "Well, I've got this job as a delivery driver for Dunning Toy Company. Now, I've had the job only a few weeks, but I really need to hang on to it. I've sort of . . . uh . . . bounced between professions for a little while, and my bills have a way of stacking up. Anyway, a few days ago, I've got a shipment of toys—rubber duckies—on my flatbed truck, and I'm on my way to drop them off at a warehouse in Hudson. I'm driving over a bridge out by Schuylerville Lake and, okay, so maybe I was going a little fast, and maybe I wasn't paying real close attention to the road, but I'll tell you one thing: that deer came out of nowhere. I swerve to avoid it, and a crate of the merchandise—a couple hundred rubber ducks—goes flying off the truck, over the bridge, and into the lake."

"So *that's* how the ducks got into Schuylerville Lake," I said.

Darrel Sullivan continued: "I pull the truck over and walk down to the shore in hopes that I can gather the ducks.

By now, they're all floating out in different directions. I waded in a little and snagged a few, but it was hopeless. I left 'em all there in the lake." He cackled in disbelief. "So you can imagine my surprise when I heard that they suddenly showed up in the Bratwurst King's backyard. I drove over there on Tuesday morning, and, sure enough, there were my duckies. I followed Officer Portnoy and watched him throw them into the shed behind the police station. I waited until it was the middle of the night, and then I went to retrieve them."

"How come you wanted them back so bad?" Shanks asked.

Darrel Sullivan sighed again. "Because as far as Dunning Toy Company knows, those ducks have been delivered. I signed and filed the paperwork that said so. Like I said, I really need this job. I had no idea *how* the ducks ended up in Babbage's yard. I figured maybe I could steal them back and deliver them to that warehouse in Hudson after all. Sure, they'd be a few days late, but nobody would know the difference."

"So you're saying that you have no idea how the duckies ended up in the middle of the Bell Woods?"

"Huh? Bell Woods?" Portnoy's eyebrows folded down with confusion.

Darrel Sullivan held out his wrists together. "I've told you everything. Now, are you going to take me downtown, Officer Portnoy, or what?"

"ATTENTION, BONANZA GUESTS!"

A voice boomed out over the loudspeakers from every corner of the festival.

"THE JUDGES HAVE SELECTED THE FIVE FINALISTS FOR THIS YEAR'S BRATWURST COOK-OFF. . . ."

I gripped Shanks's shoulder, wide-eyed with anticipation. Everyone around us froze and listened for the names. Even Portnoy and Darrel Sullivan tilted their heads toward the speakers.

"WOULD THE FOLLOWING TEAMS PLEASE REPORT TO THE STAGE FOR THE FINAL TASTE-OFF: TEAM BABBAGE . . . TEAM PHILLY RICH . . . TEAM MURF . . . TEAM MARCONI . . ."

Shanks and I went for a high five, missed, then looked around to see if anyone was watching.

". . . AND TEAM PORTNOY. THE TASTE-OFF WILL BEGIN IN FIFTEEN MINUTES."

All of us turned to Portnoy in surprise. Apparently, he'd managed to perfect that spicy bratwurst recipe after all. He seemed more stunned than any of us. In fact, for a moment I thought he might topple right over from shock. But then his face regained its composure and he looked down at Darrel Sullivan.

"Well, Mr. Sullivan, it looks like a deputy might be taking you downtown instead of me." He took his walkie-talkie from his belt and grumbled a message into it, then turned to level a stern gaze at Shanks and me.

"Say, where is your friend Pebble, anyway?" he asked.

"Peephole's at the hospital with his brand-new little sister," I said.

"Well, congratulations to him. Chunk, that's some fine detective work. And Macaroni . . . looks like I'll be seeing you in the finals. Best of luck."

Ding ding. A text from my dad.

Game time, bud! Meet us at the stage. We need you!

This was the craziest Bellwood Bratwurst Bonanza I'd ever been to. The Marconi family had made it into the finals of the cook-off, and the One and Onlys had only one suspect left.

My dad was right. It was game time.

⇒ 20 ⇐

The Last Suspect

The big stage for the cook-off finals was set up on the playing field. Shanks and I joined a river of Bellwoodians flowing toward the main event. The faces around us were bright with anticipation, and the air sang with excited voices. I glimpsed my parents at one of the five tables on-stage, busily setting up their dish. My dad cocked his head and peered out over the crowd. I knew he was looking for me, so I waved my arm at him like a wild man. He didn't see me.

"Hurry up and get on that stage," Shanks said. "You've got a Bonanza to win!"

"What about the investigation? We're so close. We only have one suspect left!"

"I know, but this is the finals. We'll confront Janice afterward. Go!"

A clump of brown mustard–colored bodies holding

instruments next to the stage caught my attention. "There she is!" I yelped, barely able to control all of the energy coursing through my body.

"Paul!" My mom had caught sight of me and was calling to me from the stage. "Can you believe it? We're in the finals! Come on up! We need you!"

I looked back at Janice. She was standing a few feet away from the rest of the band, her eyes closed, her shoulders rising and falling with her breathing. She seemed to be psyching herself up for the victory song.

It *had* to be her. There were no other suspects. Not only did Pocus not have anything to do with the ducks, he was convinced they were a love letter from beyond the grave from his deceased wife. Bella had lied to us only because she'd gone fishing instead of going to work. She was innocent of any ducky nonsense. And Darrel Sullivan had confessed to spilling the duckies in Schuylerville Lake, then breaking into the storage shed to get them back, but he said he *didn't* put the duckies in Babbage's yard. And somebody else took the duckies from the police and dumped them in the Bell Woods swamp.

Yes, I admitted to myself, Janice was at Babbage's the morning the ducks arrived. She was at the police shed the day we investigated the break-in. She was at the swamp when I discovered the duckies there. She had been at all the wrong places at just the right time. Why? What was her game? To get in Babbage's head?

I couldn't take it any longer. I had to find out right then

and there. "Just a minute," I mouthed to my mom, then turned to face the band.

"What are you doing?" Shanks said. "You're going to confront Janice *now?*" This time it was her turn to keep up with me as I marched toward a suspect.

We planted ourselves firmly in front of Janice. My entire body was tight with tension, my fingers tingling with nerves. But this had to happen. The One and Onlys were going to solve this case.

"Janice," I said as evenly as I could manage. "We've got to ask you a question."

She opened her eyes slowly and looked at us. She seemed a little surprised, but she was more than a little pale. And sweaty. She looked like she was about to cry. Or scream, maybe? Actually, she looked like she was about to puke.

"Are you okay?" That wasn't the question I had planned on asking her, but it seemed the most appropriate.

She blew out a deep breath and her eyes got wide, and I braced myself for a barf shower. Instead, she stumbled a little. Shanks lunged and caught her before she fell, and my old babysitter reached out and put a hand on my shoulder to steady herself.

"It's all right," Shanks said. "We've got you."

"Sorry," Janice said faintly, "I suddenly don't feel so well."

We carefully helped her to a sitting position on the grass, and I sat down next to her.

"I'll go get you some water," Shanks said, then dashed away.

For a second, I wondered if this was a trick of some kind. If she was the ducky thief, maybe this was an attempt to distract us, and then she'd take off, just like Darrel Sullivan. One look at her face, which was beginning to turn the same shade of green as her eyes, told me that she wasn't faking it.

"I'm so nervous about our performance," Janice said, tilting her head in the direction of the band. "Mr. Mundo, the band director, wants me to play a giant tuba instead of my regular tuba."

"What's the difference?" Shanks asked.

"It's bigger," Janice said. "And it's completely different to play. Mr. Mundo said it actually belonged to Wolfgang Munchaus, too. Apparently, the Bellwood Historical Society decided to let us play it at the last minute."

"That sounds like a huge honor," I offered.

"As if I wasn't already nervous enough," Janice said, rolling her eyes. "Plus, I think I may have eaten something funny. Did you try one of Darrel Sullivan's lobster rolls?"

"I don't think that was lobster," Shanks said, back at my side with a bottle of water.

Janice stuck her tongue out. "I don't think that was *food.*"

Shanks and I watched silently as she took small swigs of water, dabbing the sweat from her forehead with the sleeve of her band uniform. Finally, her face stopped look-ing so green.

"I'm so embarrassed," she said. "It's not just the lobster. See, I've got this stage-fright thing. It can make me a little light-headed. And I've been worrying about this moment all week. Pretty silly for a performer, huh? But the victory song is the crowning moment of the Bonanza."

"It's not silly at all," Shanks said. From the look on her face, she was as stymied as I was. Should we hammer our suspect with questions or comfort her? "Do you know how to play the song?"

Janice smiled. "Back and forth, up and down. I've been practicing all week long. Pretty much drove my parents in-sane. And in the middle of the night, when I couldn't sleep, I'd sneak out and practice some more. You'd think I'd be pretty confident right now, but I've got this giant tuba to deal with. And there are so many people here." She waved her bottle of water at the ocean of spectators.

"Did you say you 'sneak out'?" I asked.

Janice looked at me with a mischievous grin. "Want to hear something ridiculous? I couldn't play in the house be-cause I'd wake my parents up, so I went out to the middle of Bell Woods so nobody would hear me."

"I know," I said sheepishly.

Her face crinkled in confusion. "You know?"

"I . . . kinda . . . um . . . saw you out there."

"You did? What were you doing in the woods in the middle of the night?"

"Following you."

Janice stared at me, her face registering nothing at all.

"I wasn't *planning* on following you," I explained. "I was sitting outside my window because I couldn't sleep. And then I saw you sneak out of your house with your scooter and zip into the woods. I *had* to follow."

Janice's jaw seemed to tighten a little while she continued to stare at me. I tried to swallow, but my mouth was suddenly bone-dry.

And then she exploded into a laugh. "This town," she said, shaking her head, "can it get any funnier? Did you see the duckies out there?"

"Actually," I said, taking the opportunity, "we were going to ask *you* about them. Did you put them there?"

"*Me?*" She laughed even harder. "No. I couldn't believe my eyes when I saw them. It was the weirdest thing ever! You should ask Officer Portnoy about them. Maybe he'll tell you why they're out there."

"He doesn't know anything about it," Shanks said.

Janice's smile faded a little. "Are you sure? I mean, I was out there practicing on Tuesday night, and there were no duckies. Then, on my way back home, a van sped by me, heading down the forest road into the woods. In fact, it almost ran me over. It slammed on its brakes, and I swerved off the road."

The screeching noise. That's what woke me up on Tuesday night. And then I saw Janice sneaking back into her house.

"You think that Officer Portnoy was driving?" I asked.

"The headlights were too bright for me to see the driver," Janice said. "But I did get a good look at the van when it barreled into the woods. There was a big stripe across the side, and on the back doors it said 'Bellwood Police.'"

"ATTENTION, BONANZA GUESTS!" The loudspeakers attached to the stage startled us all. "THE FINAL COOK-OFF WILL NOW BEGIN!"

"Paul!" Both my parents leaned over the edge of the stage. "Game time!"

I turned back to Janice. "Gotta go. But . . . thanks for the help on the case."

Shanks gave Janice a pat on the back. "You're going to be great up there!"

Janice nodded and stood up. "Good luck, Paul. I hope it's the Marconis' Bonanza!"

21

A New Definition of "Delicious"

"What have you been doing?" my mom asked as I settled into my seat at Team Marconi's table. "I thought your dad and I were going to have to do this on our own."

"Investigating mysteries," I answered.

From the elevated stage I peered out over the familiar faces of Bellwood. There was Bella Tuff, grinning at us from the back. There was Byron Willis, and Janice's parents—even Hal the llama had a spot cleared for him. There were my neighbors, my classmates, my teachers. And there was Shanks, hustling up to the front row to sit with her parents. She spotted me onstage and flashed a thumbs-up.

Part of me was relieved. I had never wanted to believe that Janice Wagner was responsible for all the ducky hijinks, and now I knew that she *wasn't* the ducky thief. But she was the last of our suspects. Who did that leave? And what did it mean that Janice had seen a police van going into the woods? I remembered that there was a larger set of footprints at the swamp. Could those have belonged to Portnoy?

I glanced at the table to my right. Portnoy was carefully arranging his spicy bratwurst on a paper plate. His face was about an inch away from the sausage. His mustache was flecked with mayonnaise. Was he really the ducky mastermind?

"I've got a mystery for you," my dad said, pointing to Pocus at the other end of the line of contestant tables. "How is he still going to have room in his belly for our bratwurst by the time he makes it all the way down here?"

It was a good question: Team Marconi's table was fourth of five finalists. Team Murf, which consisted of Mrs. Murf and her husband (just Murf) was first up, followed by Philly Rich, a photographer for the town newspaper, the *Bellwood Noise*. After him, it was Portnoy and his spicy bratwurst, then us. The last table was Babbage, the Bratwurst King himself.

"He's sampling each dish, not actually gobbling it up," my mom said, putting the final touches on the presentation plate. "Mr. Pocus is a sausage connoisseur. I heard that he hasn't eaten anything but rice porridge and lukewarm water for the last two weeks, to prepare his taste buds for the event."

"I heard it was two months," my dad said.

My parents grasped each other's hands and looked over at Babbage, who seemed as relaxed as possible. He wasn't even looking up; he was the absolute definition of confidence, sitting back with his feet on the table, scribbling casually into a notebook. I leaned over and could make out what he was drawing: a sketch of a rubber ducky. In its little wing, it held the wiener trophy.

This was the moment some people had spent all year preparing for; others, their whole lives. This moment could make or break a person. This was the Bellwood Bratwurst Bonanza, and it was even more than that to the Marconis. This year, because of the Conquistador, my parents were worried about the family hardware store. If it did close down, a bratwurst food cart could be another way to make money. But for the plan to work, we needed to win this cook-off.

WOCK WOCK WOCK. Everybody glanced up to watch a pair of helicopters rumble by overhead. Each was dangling something below it that looked like a big orange bag.

"They're called helibuckets," my dad said, shouting over the noise. "They're filled with water. When the helicopter gets above the fire, the crew dumps the water on it. Pretty cool, huh? Wouldn't want to accidentally spill *that* bucket, would you?"

I shook my head, but I was distracted by the deafening sound of the helicopter. There was something otherworldly about the noise. Something . . . monstrous. And then I re-membered what Babbage had said to Officer Portnoy the day we discovered the duckies. He'd had a dream about a growling beast. And then he woke up to find the duckies on his lawn. His *wet* lawn.

A hush fell over the crowd. We turned to our right to see Pocus, the chief taster himself, stride confidently to the center of the stage. He stood for a moment and bowed respectfully at each of the finalists, then turned to face the audience.

"The tasting . . . ," he bellowed in a high, authoritative voice, "will now begin!"

I sprang up from my seat. "I'll be right back," I whispered to my parents, and was already scurrying across the stage before they could yank me back to my seat. Luckily, everyone was focused on Pocus, the most important man in Bellwood, and not on me.

"Psst!" I called out as I leaned over the side of the stage. *"Janice!"*

Janice's head popped into view below me. She and the rest of the band were watching the finals from the side of the stage.

"What's up?" she asked.

"What lake?" I blurted.

"Huh?"

I tried to slow down. "The other day you said that the Bellwood Fire Department was using helicopters to fight the forest fires. And they're dumping water on the fires, right?"

"That's right!"

"So do you know what lake they're getting the water from?"

"Oh." Janice smiled. "Yeah. Schuylerville Lake. Why?"

"I'll explain later! Thanks!"

I scuttled back to my seat as an approving murmur rolled through the crowd. Pocus had just approached Team Murf's table. Somebody in the back yelled out, "Babbage is king!" and a cascade of *Shh*'s, like a choir of snakes, followed from the people of Bellwood.

I tried to get Shanks's attention, but she was staring intently as Murf and Mrs. Murf introduced their entry, which was called "Bangers and Hash." It was a sweet sausage baked into hash browns, topped with fried onions and sprinkled with pickle juice. Pocus lifted the fork to his mouth, closed his eyes, and chewed once, twice, three times. He swallowed. A low rumble of excitement spread through the crowd. Finally, he bowed and thanked the Murfs for the bite and moved on to the next table.

I pulled out my phone and thumbed a quick text to Shanks.

duckies and Tina came from Schuylerville Lake +
Babbage's grass was wet. I think a fire dept helicopter
dropped them from sky!

I watched as Shanks's attention switched from Pocus to her pocket. She pulled out her phone, read my text, then looked up at me. Her eyes got wide, and her mouth formed an "O." Her thumbs tapped at her phone.

Ding ding.

By accident? Or on purpose?

I sent back three question marks.

Before sampling Philly Rich's "Frank You Berry Much" blueberry-and-bratwurst ice cream, Pocus took a big swig from a glass of water, gargled noisily for a few seconds, then spit into a bucket that an attendant had hurriedly brought onstage.

"Cleansing the palate," my mom whispered to me. "No taste from the previous dish can linger in his mouth."

I tried to clear my mind. What did it all mean? If I was right, then a fire department helicopter had picked up the duckies while collecting water from Schuylerville Lake. If the drop on Babbage's yard was an accident, why steal the duckies from the storage shed and dump them in the swamp? But if somebody dropped them from the helicopter on purpose, why Babbage's house? His next-door neighbor, Pocus, would have been a more likely target.

And why did someone who was driving a Bellwood police van dump them in the Bell Woods? But then I remembered something Byron Willis told us. The police and fire departments shared vehicles. Maybe it was someone from the fire department, not the police, who almost hit Janice with the van.

Pocus repeated the tasting ritual with Philly Rich and then with Officer Portnoy, who introduced his dish simply as "Spicy Bratwurst." I tried to read Pocus's expression after every bite, but he was a true professional. Whether he loved it or hated it, you couldn't tell. The giddiness he'd had on his face earlier after kissing Hal the llama and the serenity he'd expressed when talking about Clara were pushed back below the surface. He'd undergone an amazing transformation in the last few days—that couldn't be denied. But this was the Triple B. And business was business.

A ruckus arose from the crowd. All eyes turned to see a scampering fur ball bouncing down the aisle carrying a rubber ducky in its mouth. It looked like Wild Bill Chipmunk was making another run for it, and this time he'd found a souvenir. Several people were giving chase, but Wild Bill was not about to stop. He raced up the stairs and onto the stage, scampering by Pocus and all of the finalists. The crowd erupted with laughter. Everybody clutched each other and stood on their tippy toes to track Wild Bill's escape.

Everybody, that is, except Byron Willis. As the tallest person at the Triple B, he could see the rodent just fine. But he wasn't laughing. In fact, he had a troubled look on his face. Either he'd made the mistake of sampling Darrel Sullivan's lobster rolls or Wild Bill was the last thing on earth he wanted to see.

Eventually, Wild Bill leapt off stage right and disappeared into the row of booths, his handlers trailing him all the way. When the crowd settled itself down, it was finally Team Marconi's turn.

"We humbly present our dish: 'Swine in a Sleeping Bag,'" my mother said, her voice even and controlled.

"Oink oink!" my dad said loudly, grinning like a lunatic.

My mom and I flashed him embarrassed looks, and he shrugged. "Sorry," he mouthed to us silently. "Just nervous."

Pocus accepted the paper plate from my mom and opted to lift the pancake and brat with his hand instead of a fork. He closed his eyes and took a bite. Immediately, his eyes shot back open. He looked down at the plate in his hand and then at my parents. His eyes grew very small, then incredibly round; his nostrils flared out; his ears poked up like a startled dog; he chewed once, twice, three times, then swallowed with an exaggerated gulp. A change slowly occurred in his face, and at once I thought, *Oh, no, my parents have poisoned him.* He remained absolutely still for a second or two longer, and I thought he might tip over like a building crumbling to the ground. Then, in an instant, his face smoothed out and returned to its composed, expressionless features. I sighed with relief. At least Team Marconi wouldn't go down in history as the only finalist to kill a chief taster.

I glanced back over at Byron. I was still bothered by the face he'd made at the sight of Wild Bill. But then I wondered if it was Wild Bill that bothered him or the ducky in the rodent's mouth. Once again, I felt the nagging urge to ask him a question. I'd always felt like we'd missed something when we talked to him at the storage shed.

Finally, Pocus glided up to Babbage's table. It might have been my imagination, but I could have sworn he stood a little bit straighter, was a little more attentive in front of the long-standing champ. Babbage was sausage royalty, after all, even if the two had had their share of disputes. Babbage sat up and cordially bowed to Pocus, presenting his entry with a little flourish of the hand.

"I call this dish 'Kraut to Sea.' Here," Babbage explained, "we have a playful bed of my homemade sauerkraut, featuring my patented special sauce, and here"—his voice was measured, confident, and clear, like he was hosting his own cooking show—"poking up from under this small ocean of fermented cabbage like tiny lifeboats, we have the pearls of the dish, my grilled kielbasa morsels."

Pocus nodded appreciatively at Babbage's introduction. He carefully picked up the small paper dish and tasted the treat. He took small nibbles, and there was something gnomish about the way his lips moved.

Gnomish. Who else had compared Pocus to a gnome? Byron, I remembered, when we talked to him at the storage shed.

I closed my eyes and tried to remember the conversation.

Byron had looked genuinely surprised when he found out that the storage shed had been broken into and evidence stolen. *What would anyone want with all those duckies?* he had asked. A reasonable question. But not if nobody had mentioned that the duckies *were* the stolen evidence.

And then I remembered what else I'd been wanting to ask him.

I jabbed another text to Shanks.

Byron Willis is sitting behind you. Go ask him if he's ever been in Pocus's garden.

Shanks looked down at her phone, then looked at me. She scrunched her face up like she didn't understand.

"Just do it," I mouthed, trying not to draw attention to myself.

I glanced at my parents, who were watching Pocus closely, and noted the looks of awe, reverence, and concern on their faces. For a long minute, the only sound to be heard was Pocus's rhythmic chewing, which for some reason reminded me of ocean waves lapping against a sandy shore.

"I have come to my decision," Pocus finally said, and the crowd stirred with anticipation. "But before I name the winner of the Bonanza cook-off, I have an announcement. After today I will be stepping down as chief taster. Next year I'll be entering the contest with my own bratwurst dish!"

A gush of excited voices rippled through the audience, then hushed as Pocus raised a hand. Shanks, meanwhile, was dutifully crouch-walking two rows back, passing by people with *Excuse me*'s on her way to Byron.

"Mr. Babbage," Pocus said ceremoniously, "your 'Kraut to Sea' is a work of mastery and delight."

Babbage tried unsuccessfully to contain a self-pleased grin.

"Your entry this year is indeed inspired," Pocus continued, "and it is good enough for third place."

A collective gasp rose from the crowd. Babbage's grin stayed glued to his face, as if the chief taster had just said something in a foreign language and he was waiting for someone to translate it.

I looked out into the audience and saw that Shanks had made it to Byron's row and was now squeezing past people to get to him.

"There are two dishes this year that have pushed our annual competition to new heights," Pocus continued, turning to the crowd with the dignified presence of a Roman emperor. "One devilishly spicy, the other heavenly sweet. In second place, we have a newcomer to the competition. With his 'Spicy Bratwurst,' Officer Rutherford Portnoy has created an arresting meal that will lock up your taste buds and throw away the key."

The crowd erupted into thunderous applause, whooping and yeehaw-ing and laughing in disbelief. Shanks was

nearly knocked over in the fray, but when she got her footing, she let out a "Woo-hoo!" in the chief's honor.

Portnoy himself simply nodded and mouthed silent
Thank you's, his mustache concealing a half smile. But from
the stage, I could see that his eyes were glistening ever so
slightly with tears of joy.

"And now," Pocus said, "the moment we've all been
waiting for. . . ."

Finally, Shanks had made it to Byron's side. She tugged
at his sleeve. The tall teenager bent down as she whispered
the question in his ear.

". . . the winning recipe has given us all a new definition
of 'delicious'!" I heard Pocus say, but my eyes were glued on
Shanks and Byron.

Byron touched his ear like he couldn't hear Shanks and
bent down lower. She leaned in again and whispered in
his ear.

". . . this dish will usher in a new era of Bonanza!"

Byron straightened up, his face a mask of confusion.
"No!" he seemed to say, shaking his head. And that was
all I needed to convince me that Babbage was never the
intended target at all. Pocus was. And Byron was not only
our ducky thief, but he'd dug up Pocus's tomatoes, too.

Byron looked down at Shanks, who was looking at me.
Then Byron looked at me. We locked eyes. He must have
read it right on my face. He knew that I knew.

"Ladies and gentlemen of Bellwood," Pocus shouted,

"I give you your Bratwurst Bonanza champions . . . Team Marconi!"

The crowd went wild.

My parents went wild.

Byron went for the exit.

⇒ 22 ⇐

A Giant Tuba and Bellwood's Lankiest Kid

The band started in with "We Are the Champions," jangling and blowing and stomping and kicking out the tune, and the crowd went nutso for its new Bonanza winner, and my parents and I were in a vortex of hugs and kisses and fist bumps and high fives and back pats, and the world during those few seconds was all hair, teeth, and eyeballs, and there was a floating tangle of voices saying, "How'd ya do it?" and "How does it feel?" and "What a stunner of a bratwurst!" and it was confusing and loud and glorious, and they handed us the bratwurst trophy, and everything smelled like syrup.

I managed to wrestle free and look over the audience. Byron was trying to fight his way out of the crowd, but his long limbs were all snaggled up in the mass of celebrating bodies. He wasn't making much progress.

"Tackle him!" I shouted to Shanks, but she was getting jostled around, too.

"What?" she called back.

"Tackle him!" I yelled wildly, and my voice barely carried over all the noise.

Shanks's face went from surprise to pure excitement, and she started burrowing through bodies to get to Byron.

In the fray, I was pushed up against Babbage. Despite coming in third place, he didn't seem upset. Shocked, yes, but he was eyeing my parents with respect. Perhaps he was finally happy to have some real competition. Perhaps he was already planning his comeback at next year's Triple B.

Suddenly, Mr. Pocus sprang like a cuckoo clock in front of my parents and me. "Team Marconi," he said, extending his arm for a handshake, "I'd like to congratulate you on your victory."

Scanning the crowd again, I couldn't find Shanks or Byron. Had Byron already fled? Or were they buried somewhere in the party? I did notice that most everybody seemed to be looking at the stage with puzzled expressions. I turned to see what they were ogling and spotted Janice at the front of the stage, straining mightily over her tuba. She was blowing and blowing, but no sound was coming out. Her face was getting so red, it looked like she was about to pass out cold right in the middle of the celebration.

Slowly the noise of the celebration dimmed until everybody was quietly watching Janice struggle with her giant instrument. The other band members had stopped playing. They just stood back, staring at her.

"There's something stuck in the tuba!" Chad Foster shouted.

Janice must have come to the same conclusion, because she laid the tuba on the ground and reached into the bell. But her hand came back empty.

"Her arms aren't long enough to reach whatever is in there!" I shouted. And then an idea struck me. This reminded me of a story I'd just heard.

"It's like Waffle the Dolphin!" I exclaimed to nobody in particular.

"And the world's tallest man," Peephole answered, appearing at my side out of nowhere in the chaos of the celebration.

"Peephole! Where did you come from?"

But he didn't respond. He had a strange look on his face, a look I'd never seen before. Usually, he looked annoyed, bored, or scared, or some combination of those three. But now his eyes were clear and fixed, his jaw was straight, his back was rigid. He looked determined and . . . fearless. This was his moment to help.

"And since the world's tallest man isn't here," he said, "I'll have to give it a shot."

I watched him stride confidently across the stage. He moved quickly, not frantically, as he rolled his T-shirt sleeve up to his shoulder, bent down on one knee, and stuck his arm down inside the tuba.

"You can do it, Peephole!" I shouted.

It seemed like eons, but it was only seconds, while Peephole reached farther and farther into the tuba.

Then his face fell. "I can't do it. There's something in there, but my arms aren't long enough." He stood and looked out at the crowd. Suddenly, he pointed his finger at the back row. "Byron! Byron Willis!" He shouted, and everybody's head swung around to look.

Byron was at the edge of the crowd, slowly moving away from the stage. Something was dragging from his legs. It was Shanks.

"Byron!" Peephole shouted again. "We need your help!"

The tallest teenager in Bellwood froze. All eyes were now on him. He seemed to consider his options for a second, then realized he didn't have many. He straightened himself, shook his legs free of Shanks's badgerlike grip, and strolled up to the stage.

Somebody started clapping as he took the stage, and then everybody else joined in. His face turned red as he bent down over the tuba, peered in, then reached his long, noodlelike arm into the horn. The crowd cheered him on as he reached and reached.

His face lit up. He had found something! Straining, he wrenched his arm back and forth. Janice bent down and started blowing into the mouthpiece again, as if the wind might jostle the object loose. At last, Byron yanked his arm free and held up the thing that had been plugging Janice's tuba.

Janice's giant tuba blew out a long, low note. The crowd stopped clapping and fell silent. And Byron stared at the rubber ducky clutched in his hands, the word "Confess" written across its back. The tuba seemed to ring out forever. When it finally stopped, Byron filled the silence with a barbaric yawp.

"I confess!" he shrieked. "I dropped the duckies! I stole them from the shed! It was me! Me! Me!"

Imagine a gallery of blinking, confused faces. Everybody in Bellwood stared at Byron, trying to process his frantic confession.

Everybody, that is, except my dad, who was concentrating so hard on his victory shimmy that he didn't notice the scene at all. He was doing his flaming-pajamas dance, which was appropriate, it turns out, because behind him the table was on fire.

In the excitement of winning, we'd forgotten to turn the griddle off, and now the tablecloth was sending up flames into the air. A circle formed around the table, with a lot of people pointing and shouting for somebody to do something, but nobody did anything. Burning down the Triple B would have definitely put a damper on our victory celebration.

In an instant Byron Willis transformed from villain to hero, launching across the stage in a somersault roll. With a swift tug he unplugged my dad's griddle, then bounced to his feet, swiped the cloth from Portnoy's table, and smothered the fire. With long, fluid steps he ran to the edge of the stage and plucked up a fire extinguisher. In a few quick seconds he'd swept the spray across the flames and reduced the fire to a soggy, sooty mess.

The crowd burst into applause, but Byron didn't acknowledge it. Instead, he threw the extinguisher aside and bounded after Peephole, who was teetering on the edge of the stage and squawking, "I'm on fire!" though he obviously wasn't.

Byron tackled him anyway. They rolled around on the stage, looking like two rubber bands locked in a championship wrestling match.

"He's attacking Peephole!" Shanks yelled from the edge of the stage.

"No! He's helping him!" I said. "See?"

Byron gathered himself to his feet and extended his arm to help Peephole up. The two of them surveyed their arms and legs. No fire.

Shanks and I raced to Peephole's side.

"You're the ducky mastermind!" Shanks barked at Byron, then her tone softened. "But . . . you saved Peephole. Er, you *would* have saved him if he'd actually been on fire. So . . . uh . . . thanks?"

The bashing of a bass drum made us jump, and we turned to see the victory band start again from the top, this time in full force with Janice's tuba. "We Are the Champions" rang out over the Triple B, and the crowd came alive again with dancing and cheering.

Portnoy appeared at our side, the newly pinned

second-place ribbon on his uniform. "Well, kids . . . I'd say it's been a heck of a Bonanza. Why don't we go find ourselves a quiet place to sit and talk this out?"

"You got it, chief!" Shanks said, and she gave him a salute.

He winked, but he didn't return the salute.

⇒ 23 ⇐

The Last Confession

"I never want to see another rubber ducky as long as I live," Byron said. He was sitting on a patch of grass away from the noise of the Bonanza celebration, hugging his bony knees to his chest. Shanks, Peephole, Portnoy, and I all sat around him.

"I thought I might be able to get away with the whole thing," he continued. "I wanted to move on and forget about it, but everywhere I look there's a ducky. In front of me. Behind me. To my side. In a dang *tuba.*" He gave a frustrated little tug to his stringy bun of red hair. "I couldn't take it anymore."

Shanks reached out and pinched my arm. "I guess your plan was brilliant after all," she whispered. "When did you put the ducky in the tuba?"

"What? I thought *you* did," I replied.

"Well, Byron, you've caused quite the stir in our little town," Portnoy said, shifting his weight from side to side as he tried to get comfortable. It wasn't working. "These three detectives have run all over Bellwood to track you down. And even if they hadn't figured you out, I would have soon enough."

The One and Onlys exchanged quick glances. That was doubtful, but we kept our mouths shut.

A sudden swell of cheering came from the Bonanza crowd, and we looked over to see my dad doing his twenty-pound-marlin dance while Chad Foster played a groovy tune on the trombone. My mom was dancing the tango with a rubber ducky.

Byron let out a little groan and bent his head between his knees.

"So go ahead, Byron," Shanks said after a little while.

He looked up at her. "Go ahead what?"

"Go ahead and explain yourself. This is the part where you fill in all the details of your crime. Haven't you ever read a detective novel?"

Byron considered this for a moment. "I'd rather not."

"Chunk is right," Portnoy chimed in. "I think you owe us an explanation. Besides, I've got to know what you did in order to know what to do with you."

Byron looked like he was about to protest. He opened his mouth to speak, but instead he sighed and patted the bun of hair on his head. "Okay. Well. I guess it started when I was up in the firefighting chopper."

"The helicopter?" Peephole asked.

"Yeah, the helicopter. I've been doing these training pickups and dumps for the last week or so. Out to Schuylerville Lake to pick up water, and then over to the open space below Highway 43 to dump it. I begged my mom to let me be in charge on a real flight out to the fire, but she said I had to prove I knew how to handle the equipment first. So every training run we pass over the center of Bellwood, and every run I look down on Mr. Pocus's house. He's always out there, working on his tomato garden. Every time I see him I get angry, because I'm reminded of all the grief he gave me. He used to torment me all the time, and I don't know, I just . . ."

"You don't have to explain that to me," Peephole said. "I completely understand."

"But this one morning, I look down from the chopper and he's not there. His tomato plants are out there all alone, unprotected. And then something comes over me. I blacked out for a second with rage, and as we passed by overhead, I flipped the switch to dump the water. Seven hundred and eighty gallons. I wanted to ruin those stupid tomatoes of his. But because I had been so distracted all morning, I didn't realize that we'd picked up the duckies in the lake. Well, I completely missed Pocus's yard altogether."

"And you hit Babbage's instead," I said.

He nodded.

"But didn't anybody see what you had done? What about the helicopter pilot?" Shanks asked.

Byron shrugged. "Felix is the oldest pilot in the department. He knows his way around a helicopter, but he's half deaf and not the most observant. He didn't notice when we dumped nothing but air over the field. Anyway, after the chopper run, I booked it over to Babbage's, but there was already a crowd gathering. And that's when I started freaking out."

"Why?" Shanks asked.

"Because I thought that Officer Portnoy might take the duckies back to the station, and my mom might see them, and she might be curious and ask questions and then figure out that I'd dumped them, which is a horrible misuse of the department equipment. Not only would she never allow me to go on a *real* mission, she'd probably kick me off the Junior Firefighters. . . . But I live for the Junior Firefighters."

"So you broke into the storage shed and removed the duckies?" Peephole asked.

Byron's long fingers spread out in front of him. "It's not really breaking in if I have the key," he said. "Still, I knew it was wrong. I told myself that I wasn't getting rid of evidence—I was moving it to a place where nobody would ever find it."

"We found it," Shanks said.

"Yeah, I figured that out as soon as I saw the duckies all over the Bonanza. There was even one on the fire department's sign-up table. How could I have known the Bell

Woods would suddenly be such a hot spot? I almost hit somebody on the old forest road."

"That was Janice Wagner," I said. "There's still one thing I don't get. Why'd you go back and tear up Mr. Pocus's tomato plants?"

"How'd you know that was me?" Byron asked, real curiosity in his voice. He seemed like he was almost relieved to have confessed.

"When we talked to you at the storage shed," I explained, "you said that Pocus reminded you of one of his garden gnomes. But there's a big fence between Pocus's garden and Babbage's backyard, and we couldn't see any part of his garden from where we were talking on Tuesday morning. Only someone who has been in Pocus's garden would know he had gnomes back there, but you told Shanks you'd never been to Pocus's house. That's what gave you away."

Everybody, even Byron, looked impressed with my detective work. "I wasn't planning on doing it," he said, "but when I saw Pocus grinning over his fence at the duckies, something about his face just got to me. I snuck back over there later and tore the tomatoes out, which was pretty stupid. I guess I owe him an apology, not that he'll accept it."

"The old Pocus wouldn't," I said. "Who knows? I have a feeling that he's a changed man."

"Officer Portnoy," Byron said, gathering himself to his full height. "I'm ready to face justice. Can I ask one favor?"

"What's that?" Portnoy asked.

"My mom is out fighting what's left of the big fire now. Can I explain myself to her first? I think I owe it to her."

"Come on," Portnoy said, escorting Byron by the arm, "let's give her a call from the station."

Portnoy led Byron a few steps toward the crowd, then halted and turned back to us. He raised a flat hand to the brim of his hat. A real salute.

We returned it. The One and Onlys, Bellwood's official unofficial junior detective force, had solved the case of the mysterious duckies.

"I think I sat in chipmunk poop," Peephole said, twisting around to get a better view of the seat of his shorts.

Shanks and I fell to the grass, laughing.

"Peephole! I can't believe you're here!" I said.

"Did you run away again?" Shanks asked, cringing.

"Not this time." Peephole shook his head. "I begged my parents to let me go to the Triple B. I told them I had important business to take care of."

"I can't believe our luck," I said. "You showed up at the perfect moment. If you'd been able to pull the ducky out of Janice's tuba yourself, Byron would have escaped."

"Luck had nothing to do with it," he said with a wink. "Who do you think put that ducky in there to begin with?"

"*You?*" Shanks and I yowled in unison.

Peephole's face flushed with a proud grin. "This chipmunk in a cowboy hat dropped it at my feet as I was walking up toward the stage. It gave me an idea. I stuffed it way down there right before the band went onstage, when everybody was watching Pocus announce the winner. I knew that Byron was the only person with arms long enough to reach it."

"But . . . how did you know that he was the ducky thief?" I asked.

"You kept saying that you felt like we missed something at the storage shed. So as I was sitting next to Trill this morning, I went back in my memory to that day. I remembered that Janice's shoes were really muddy, even though Bellwood was in a drought. It made sense once we found out she'd been in the swamp. There was another set of footprints out there—somebody with bigger feet. And that's when I saw it in my memory of the storage shed. Byron shut his locker right as we started talking to him. Before he did, I caught a glimpse of them stuffed in there: a pair of muddy sneakers. Once I remembered that, everything fell into place. I knew that Byron had to be our ducky mastermind."

"Wow," I said. "Not bad at all, Peephole."

"Wait, wait, wait." Shanks waved her hands in front of her. "You're telling me that you touched a rubber ducky that had been in a chipmunk's mouth?"

Peephole smiled casually. "I'm a big brother now. I can't be afraid of dumb things like that."

The three of us looked at the crowd, which was now a

full-on dance party. Janice was spinning around her giant tuba, Chad Foster was doing the funky chicken, and Pocus was two-stepping across the stage. Yep. Just another ordinary day in Bellwood.

"Well, now what?" Shanks asked.

I grinned. "Who's hungry for some victory bratwurst?"

⇒ 24 ⇐

A View from Above

A few days after the Bonanza, my parents got a phone call from Officer Portnoy. He congratulated them on their victory and said that it was an honor to come in second place to such rising stars of the sausage world. And then he asked to talk to me.

"Macaroni, I wanted to congratulate you, too," he said, his gravelly voice sounding like it was coming from the bottom of a bowl of clam chowder.

"Call me Paul," I said. "And thanks, chief, but it was mostly my parents who made the recipe."

"I meant on the ducky case. You and your friends figured it all out. Impressive stuff. Sorry I doubted you."

"We work pretty well as a team," I said. "Is Byron going to jail?"

"No. Mr. Pocus decided not to press charges over the

destruction of his tomato plants. He mentioned something about a 'new perspective.' I think maybe the old man has lost it."

"What about stealing the ducks from the storage shed? Isn't that tampering with evidence or something?"

"Well, it would be, except the ducks weren't officially evidence, because dumping duckies on somebody's lawn isn't a crime. And as Byron said, he didn't break into the storage shed. He had a key, and access to the shed."

"So he didn't commit any crimes at all?" I asked, dumbfounded.

"Oh, he committed at least one crime. By dumping all those duckies at the swamp, he was littering. He'll be doing community service for a nice long while. Also, his mom kicked him out of the fire department. At least for now. So anyway, Paul, I figured I owe you guys for helping me solve this one. Okay"—he coughed—"for *completely* solving it. What can I do to repay you?"

An idea suddenly occurred to me, but it was a long shot. "How well do you know Chief Willis?"

"We went to high school together. I respect her as much as possible for a member of the fire department."

"Do you think you could ask her to arrange something for me? Well, me and a few of my friends . . ."

WOCK WOCK WOCK. The sound of the helicopter blades was deafening. Luckily, Chief Willis gave us big earmuff headphones that blocked the noise and connected us to the radio system. She checked that our harnesses were fully fastened, then gave the thumbs-up to the pilot.

She and her fire crew were making runs back and forth from Schuylerville Lake to the front of the fire all day, and she had agreed to take us along for one dump. After much pleading and lengthy phone conversations with the chief, our parents agreed, too.

As we lifted slowly into the air, Shanks and I peered out the open door of the helicopter at the helibucket, uncoiling its rope, then rising into the air below us. Peephole kept his eyes closed tight, muttering a prayer to the helicopter gods. He had required a lot of convincing before agreeing to come along for the ride (almost as much as our parents), and now he was clearly second-guessing his decision. Janice Wagner hadn't needed any convincing. She had been waiting for this moment all summer. She flashed me an electric grin and a thumbs-up as we drifted farther away from the launching pad.

Peephole's face began to lose color. I nudged Shanks, who was taking in the view while munching on a mouthful of pretzel sticks. Normally, the chief said, food wasn't allowed in the chopper, but Shanks had convinced her that we'd need "firefighting snacks." When Shanks looked over at me, I pointed to Peephole.

Shanks gulped down the pretzels with a mighty effort, then shouted, "Is she as big as a toaster?"

"Huh?" Peephole looked up for the first time.

"Trillium," Shanks said. "Is she as big as a toaster? Or a shoe?"

"That depends," Peephole replied, his shoulders relaxing a little. "Kid shoe or adult shoe?"

"Kid shoe."

"Bigger."

"World's tallest man's shoe?"

"Much smaller."

"Could she fit in a cowboy hat?"

Peephole looked annoyed. It was working. "Why would you want to fit her in a cowboy hat?"

"I don't *want* to put her in a cowboy hat. I'm asking if you *could* put her in a cowboy hat."

"I'm not answering that question because it's so dumb."

"Loaf of bread?"

"I'm not hungry."

"No, I'm asking if she's as big as a loaf of bread."

"That depends. Wheat or white?"

"What's the difference?" I interjected. "They're the same size!"

Peephole thought about this. "Technically, I guess. But wheat feels bigger, doesn't it? Anyway, yeah, she's about the size of a small loaf of bread."

"Trillium Calloway: The Amazing Wonder Bread Baby," Shanks said, as if reading a headline.

"Your friends are funny, Pauly Sweet," Janice said, laughing.

"*Pauly Sweet?*" Peephole and Shanks said together. They looked at each other like they'd both won the lottery. I'd probably never be just Paul again.

I'd always wondered what Bellwood looked like from above, and now I was getting the chance to find out. The ride out to Schuylerville Lake went by in a flash. Below us, the full tops of green trees blobbed the landscape, reminding me of the broccoli stalks that I avoided on my dinner plate. The swimming pools of the gridded residential neighborhoods soon transformed into ponds and lakes, and then Schuylerville Lake appeared, reflecting the fuzzy morning sun in the smoke-brown sky like a giant mirror laid flat on the earth. We dipped the helibucket carefully into the water, and the downdraft from the helicopter sent out ripples across the surface. Now that we had our ammunition, it was time to head for the fire.

We could see the smoke rising into the air from a long distance away. *So you're the one causing all this trouble,* I thought.

"The fire is now ninety percent contained." Chief Willis's voice crackled through our headphones. "That means that most of it can't spread anymore. Now it's a matter of finishing the job."

The helicopter tilted toward the flames that were flicking up from the pointed tops of the forest's pine trees. Below us, as far as we could see, were the charred-black remains of the trees and landscape.

"Everything is burned," Shanks said, sadness in her voice.

"This was a big one," Chief Willis agreed. "You want to know something cool? The fire ate up so many trees that the canopy of the forest is gone. This means that more sunlight can get to the ground now. And more sunlight means that new seedlings can grow. So, yes, a lot of the forest was burned in the fire—but think of all the *new* life that will now grow out of it."

For the first time Peephole cautiously leaned over for a glance below.

"Ready with that thing?" Chief Willis motioned at the release button for the helibucket. "Ten seconds until we let it go."

The helicopter swooped lower, the smoke rising up into our lungs. "And . . . NOW!"

Janice pressed the button. We all watched as a massive spray of water poured onto the flames below. Steam shot up into the air as we zoomed away.

Before landing back in the field near the fire station, the helicopter hovered over Bellwood for a few minutes. Finally, I got my view from above. There were the interconnected roads, like the arteries of our town, where we raced on our bikes. There was Babbage's lawn, where the little ducks first appeared, and there was my house, off in the distance. There was Honest Hardware and its parking lot—the future home of my parents' bratwurst food cart. There was the field where my parents had finally won the Bonanza and where Peephole proved his detective skills. And there was the old drive-in, the place that used to hold so much magic, being transformed into a Conquistador before our very eyes. The field was about to sprout glossy aisles filled with pink plastic toys, and the edge of the woods where the One and Onlys used to meet would soon be a slick black parking lot marked with diagonal lines. I looked down at the brick and cement block piles littering the once-wild field. There were wooden stakes jabbed into the field like it was a vampire that wouldn't be killed.

Bellwood was changing, it was true, but I was starting to understand that change didn't have to be scary. I thought of Mr. Pocus's new smiling face, and Trillium, and the Bonanza trophy in our living room. Yes, some things were gone forever. But I couldn't help but be excited to see what would grow up in their place.

⇒ 25 ⇐

New Life

As Trillium drank more milk, ounce by ounce, day by day, growing bigger in the hospital, the Calloways were getting ready for her. Peephole and his dad finished converting the study into a nursery, complete with what looked like dragons but what Peephole said were flying ponies painted on the walls. Peephole's mom, getting stronger and stronger every day, finally finished a quilt to hang in the room.

Trill came home on a bright, sunny morning in late August. The Calloways had a small party in their backyard to celebrate. When my parents and I arrived, Peephole greeted us at the door with his little sister in his arms, pride and confidence radiating from his face, as if he were showing us a trophy he'd won or an ancient treasure he'd discovered. Trill was even smaller than I imagined she'd be, despite the fact that she'd gained almost two full pounds since the day she was born.

I was struck by how different Peephole seemed. He was quick to smile and laugh. He was constantly whispering into Trill's ear, even though he knew she had no idea what he was telling her. Being a big brother suited him; it gave him a responsibility, and he seemed to have lost a lot of his fear and anxiety. When the cake was passed around, though, he did wonder out loud whether one could be allergic to icing and not know it, and whether such an icing allergy might result in facial swelling or hives.

Watching Peephole hold Trill above his head, laughing and making wacky faces, then passing her gingerly over to Shanks, who took her turn making wacky faces, made me realize that the best thing that ever happened to the One and Onlys was *no longer being* the One and Onlys.

The next day the Honest Bratwurst food cart officially raised its window for business, and my mom and I spent the morning grilling up sausages and serving them to a small but steady stream of customers, while my dad manned the hardware store and sent shoppers our way. Ronald did his part by lapping up any morsels that fell on the pavement. The truck was hot and a bit cramped, with my mom and me swerving around each other (each in an I'M THE WIENER! T-shirt), the oldies were cranking from the radio in the corner, and the sweet smell of butter and syrup filled the air.

Portnoy stopped by to have lunch. He enjoyed his first

Swine in a Sleeping Bag so much that he ordered another. "Now, this is a champion bratwurst," he said, syrup dripping from his mustache onto his uniform.

At three in the afternoon, my mom told me to clock out for the day, and I hung up my apron and biked home. I was late to meet Shanks and Peephole at our new secret headquarters, but I didn't feel like riding my bike there. Nope. Today, I was going to arrive in style.

Riding on the GrassMaster 3000 was like strapping an engine to a cloud and cruising around the heavens. The machine purred like a kitten and cornered like a dream. There were three speeds, each indicated by a small picture next to the gearshift: tortoise, squirrel, and hare. I started on squirrel for a few loops before slamming it up to hare, letting the wind blow through my hair as I zipped and zapped my way across our property, cackling like a mad scientist as I zoomed toward the forest service road at the end of Munchaus Avenue.

That's right. Earlier that morning, my dad finally came to his senses and gave me permission to use the Cadillac of lawn-maintenance vehicles.

"Paul," he said, putting a hand on my shoulder, "today you become a man. Or at least close to it." And that's when he handed me the keys. I'd never felt such lawn-related excitement in all my life.

Of course, I think he meant for me to mow the grass with it, not drive it a quarter of a mile away down a dirt road to a swamp. But can you blame a guy for being enthusiastic?

I settled to a stop at our new headquarters. It was far enough out of town that nobody would find it, and it was guarded by an army of little rubber warriors, stacked in a pile with the hand-carved ONE AND ONLYS sign placed on the top.

Shanks and Peephole sat on tree stumps a small distance from the duckies, away from the mud—Peephole's idea, of course. They greeted me with a salute. I sat down on an empty stump.

"I heard you have to run a mile every day," Shanks was saying, "and if you don't do it fast enough, you don't get to eat lunch."

"Really?" Peephole looked nauseous.

"Yup. And I heard that you have to write ten-page papers every week."

"Ten pages?" Peephole asked. He was definitely pale.

"And they don't serve cupcakes for dessert anymore at lunch. They only have kale pudding or seaweed shakes."

"Kale pudding?" Peephole looked like he was perched on the edge of a vomit explosion.

"What are you talking about?" I asked.

"Sixth grade," Peephole said. "It sounds like it's going to be rough."

"Nah," I said. "Every year we think school's going to be harder, but we always get used to it, don't we?"

"Pauly Sweet is right," Shanks said. "There's nothing to be afraid of. Well, there's *lots* to be afraid of—"

"Like kale pudding," Peephole interjected.

"—but at least we've got each other's backs, right?"

"Right," I said. "And we've got to set good examples for Trill. Hey, Peephole, what do you think she's going to be when she grows up?"

"I bet she'll be an astronaut," Shanks said immediately, tossing a rock into the mud in front of us. It went *gloop.* "She'll do something cool, like become the first human to sneeze on Mars."

"Astronaut? She can't go two hours without pooping in her diapers."

"She's got some time to figure it out," I said.

We stared beyond the duckies into the thick forest of trees and lush green growth. We sat there in silence for a few minutes, thinking back on the most interesting summer we'd ever had. There were rubber ducks appearing out of nowhere, and fish flopping in the limbs of trees. There was the world's tallest man and Bellwood's littlest sister. There were telltale bath toys in giant tubas, ruined tomato gardens, and megastores blooming in empty fields. There was bratwurst and wildfires and llama-smooching grouches. There were investigations that revealed that the most mysterious people in our town were just like us: human. This was the summer that the weirdness had come to Bellwood, and I loved every minute of it.

Now, the only thing for the One and Onlys to do was sit back and wait for the next case to drop from the sky. Something told me it wouldn't be long at all.

Acknowledgments

This book truly was a collaborative project, and I owe a debt of gratitude to so many people who helped it along on its journey to publication.

To my agent, Penelope Burns: your passion, patience, tenacity, and keen eye willed this book to life. I've said it before, and I'll say it again: you helped me make a dream come true, and I couldn't have done it without you.

To my editor, Julia Maguire, and the Knopf Books for Young Readers team: your editorial wisdom helped crack the mysteries of the story for me. Thank you for believing in this book and for working so hard to make it the best it could be.

Thank you to the Northwest Academy community for inspiring me daily, and to David Schonfeld for all the commiseration. Also thanks to the Globe Foundation and the Creative Production grant for allowing me more time and resources to work on this book.

Thank you to Steven Millhauser, Kathryn Davis, Tom Bissell, and all my teachers who modeled the writing life and pushed me to get better.

To my friends who read early versions of this and other books: your feedback and excitement have been invaluable to me.

To the Shapiro family, thank you for your support. And especially to Sondra (Nana), for being my unofficial publicist.

To my parents, Harry and Lynda, and my siblings, Jen, Adam, and Rachael: thank you for your love and encouragement, and for making my childhood just strange enough to give me inspiration. And to Jack, Riley, Eli, and Charlie for keeping the strangeness alive.

And finally, to Anna, my first reader and biggest fan, and Leo: I owe you more than I could ever say. You make it all worthwhile.

About the Author

When he's not teaching high school English, Doug Cornett enjoys playing Ping-Pong, solving mysteries, and rooting for the Cleveland Cavaliers. Originally from Hudson, Ohio, Doug lives with his wife and son in Portland, Oregon. *Finally, Something Mysterious* is his debut novel.

@MrDougCornett